D1098112

THE HAUNTED STARS

The Haunted Stars

By Edmond Hamilton

IT MEANT little to young Robert Fairlie, a serious and dedicated philologist, that in this year 1966 the United States and Soviet Russia were contentious about the Moon. He had little interest in the first two rocket landings on the moon, and the bases that the two nations had built there. He knew nothing at all of the shattering discovery that the Americans had made there.

For what had been found was of such explosive potentialities that it had to be kept top-secret—the discovery that space had already been conquered long ago by races who had once spanned the stars. So that men who had expected to spend decades in reaching the nearest planet, found suddenly in their hands the way to the wider universe.

Fairlie, drawn unexpectedly because of his special knowledge into this greatest of secrets, finds that a guarded New Mexico rocket-base is only the first step of the way. That way leads out amid the unexplored stars to the lost heartworld of those space-conquerors of long ago. And it leads Fairlie and others into the appalling reality of stellar space still haunted by the past cosmic struggle whose scale in space and time dwarfs the rivalries of tiny Earth's quarreling nations.

To

Jack Williamson

who knows the starways.

THE HAUNTED STARS

by

Edmond Hamilton

A Torquil Book

DISTRIBUTED BY
DODD, MEAD & COMPANY
New York

PRINTED IN THE UNITED STATES OF AMERICA

1

MUCH LATER, Robert Fairlie was to remember the simple act of boarding the evening plane at Boston airport as the moment when he first began to move into a new, frightening universe. But at the time, it seemed to him only a pleasing break in his quiet academic routine.

Right after take-off, he opened the newspaper he had bought in the terminal. He spared only a glance at the front page, with its headline of SOVIET ACCUSES U.S. OF VIOLATING MOON AGREEMENT. He was not much interested in that continuing controversy—the Russians had been blustering about something or other ever since World War Two ended, more than twenty years ago. He went through the inner pages, searching the columns.

"Of course," he thought a bit self-consciously, "there's likely to be nothing about me at all. But there might be."

There was. But it was only a paragraph buried opposite the woman's page, and it misspelled his name. It informed that Doctor Robert Farley, professor of linguistics at Massachusetts University and noted authority on Carian "hieroglyphics"—he winced at that word—had been called to Washington to assist the Smithsonian Institution in a matter of philological research.

Not much, Fairlie thought disappointedly. But a newspaper wasn't very important. There would be more about it in the *Journal of Philological Studies*. For a young scholar—thirty-three was young, in his field—it was a thing that would definitely add prestige.

"Chap I met down at the Smithsonian," he could casually say at faculty meetings, "was telling me . . ."

He wondered what the Smithsonian had for him to do. They had merely written that his work on the Carian inscriptions had convinced them he could aid them, and would he make arrangements for a temporary substitute and come down and consult? He would, and he had. Teaching bored sophomores Grimm's Law was easily left when there was prospect of real research.

Night came, and Fairlie put down the newspaper. The passenger beside him, a middle-aged businessman by the look of him, nodded down at the headline and said, "We ought to just tell those bastards to shove it."

Fairlie, reluctant to be drawn into an exchange of cliches, said, "Perhaps you're right."

"Sure I'm right," said the other. "Everything that happens, they yell warmonger at us. Berlin, and then Suez, and now this Gassendi business. What the hell is it to them *what* we do in Gassendi?"

His voice droned on, and presently Fairlie closed his eyes and pretended to doze. Then he did doze, until a stewardess touched his shoulder and said they were coming down into Washington airport.

When Fairlie walked down the steps from the plane, he hastily scrambled into his topcoat. A raw March wind was driving across the airport and had scoured the starry sky clean and glistening. He went into the bright crowded terminal and was starting for his luggage when a man came up to him and held out his hand.

"Mr. Fairlie? I'm Owen Withers, representing the Smithsonian."

Fairlie felt surprised, and then flattered. "I didn't imagine anyone was going to meet me."

Withers smiled faintly. He was a vaguely dusty-looking little man of perhaps forty who looked like a small-town lawyer.

8

"You're more important than you realize. I'll see to your suitcase. And I have a car."

The car was a dark sedan and Withers drove it expertly away from the terminal amid a herd of taxicabs and against a cataract of headlights in the other lane. Presently he turned off that heavily travelled highway onto a peripheral boulevard. They were not going now toward the glow of downtown Washington, but Fairlie assumed that the other was taking a less congested route.

His assumption was shattered when Withers said casually, "Yes, we were lucky enough to get you a ride right out there, so you won't have to stop over in Washington at all."

Fairlie turned and stared at him. "A ride out where?"

"Why, out to New Mexico," said Withers. "Where your work will be."

"No one told me that!"

It was Withers' turn to look surprised and a little dismayed. "They didn't? Oh, Lord—another example of bureaucratic bumbling."

"But why New Mexico?" Fairlie asked. "Why does the Smithsonian want me to go out there?"

Withers made a shrugging movement without taking his hands off the wheel. "I don't know—I'm just administrative hired help. All I know is that it's a field study project."

Then he added, "Here we are."

In the darkness off the road was a far-flung pattern of lights, and a tower with many lights on it. A high fence of chain-link closed all this away from the road, and Withers was turning into an entrance that had a small guardhouse. He stopped, and a serious-faced young man in uniform came out and looked at the papers Withers handed to him.

"Okay, you can go right on through to the flight line," he said.

Withers drove on through the gate.

"What is this—an Air Force field?" asked Fairlie.

Withers nodded. "That's right. As I said, we were lucky enough to hitch you a ride on an AF plane going out there tonight.

Saves your time, and our money. Our appropriation isn't unlimited, you know."

He drove past a long, low building and onto the dark tarmac. Fairlie looked around. He had never been in a military installation before and he found it confusing. He had always imagined a great uproar of planes landing and taking off, but it was not like that. There were the lights stretching far away in lines, and an occasional small jet dark and silent on the flight line, and not much else.

He felt upset. He had expected a visit to the Institution tomorrow, a quiet office, a leisurely discussion with fellow scholars. Instead, in the most offhand fashion, he was to be passed on to New Mexico, where probably some problem in Indian languages was all there was. Whatever it was, Fairlie thought resentfully, they might have made sure somebody told him. It seemed like sloppy procedure for a scientific institution.

Withers stopped the car near another of the small planes. Fairlie was vague about airplane types, but this looked like a fast jet. There were lights near it, and a mechanic in a coverall was going away from it, wiping his hands.

"This is it," said Withers. "I'll take your suitcase."

Fairlie stared. "This plane? But I thought—"

"Get you out there in just a few hours," Withers assured him heartily. "It's an R-404—a reconnaissance job going west with an empty seat." And as a man came down out of the plane, "Ah, here's Captain Kwolek. Captain, Mr. Fairlie."

Fairlie felt a revulsion. Good Lord, this was one of those crazy tin skyrockets that went hooting and screaming across the sky at insane speeds. He didn't want to ride a thing like this. He mentally damned Withers for being so helpful about getting him a ride.

But both Withers and Kwolek seemed to take it all as a matter of course. Probably people down here in Washington thought nothing of casually jetting out to New Mexico, or to Formosa or England, on a March midnight. Captain Kwolek, a broad-faced young man with a button nose, gave him a hard handshake and an appraising stare that made Fairlie suddenly conscious of his own lank, weedy and undynamic appearance. He stifled the protest he had been about to make. His male vanity wouldn't permit him to look scared.

"Thanks for giving me a lift, Captain," said Fairlie, with what he hoped was a convincingly casual air.

"No trouble," said Kwolek. "Climb up, will you? I'll take that case. So long, Mr. Withers."

Fairlie climbed up, catching his foot once on the tail of his topcoat and feeling like a fool, and poked and scrambled into a bewilderingly crowded interior that smelled of oily metal. Another young man in uniform, dark and good-looking and tough-looking, came deftly back and helped Fairlie squeeze into a bucket-seat beside which was an odd metal framework.

"I'm Lieutenant Buford," he told Fairlie. "Here you are—better strap right in. This is the photog's seat but we're running without Charlie tonight."

That meant very little to Fairlie. He had trouble getting the strap around his topcoat, and meanwhile Kwolek was squeezing past him and taking one of the seats up front.

Presently a hellish roar exploded and Fairlie would have jumped erect if it had not been for the strap. He peered out the window but they were not moving. Kwolek did something with his hands and the roar lessened. The pilot turned and said, "We'll get clearance in a minute, Mr. Fairlie."

"Oh, yes," said Fairlie. He felt angry because they treated him like a nervous elderly passenger on a transport. He was only six or seven years older than they were, at most, and while this was all new to him . . .

The roar became loud again and the plane lurched and Fairlie felt things happen to the pit of his stomach. He clutched the camera-standard beside his seat and tried to look unconcerned. He was damned if he would let these two tough young men patronize him. They went up fast, the lights dropping away, and oddly the roar seemed to diminish as the plane ripped through the night on the leading edge of its own screeching fury.

Kwolek looked back again, and raised his voice. "All right?"

11

Fairlie nodded. "All right." After a moment he asked, "Where do we land in New Mexico?"

"Morrow Base," said Kwolek, without turning.

Fairlie stared at the back of a neck and cap that were all he could see of the pilot. After a moment, he said, "There must be some mistake."

Kwolek shrugged. "No mistake."

But there was! Fairlie thought. He knew about Morrow Base. The whole world did. It was that area of arid land in New Mexico from which the rockets of the American lunar expedition had risen, and from which the supply rockets still went out to the base in Gassendi. And it was a guarded place. It had been said that it would be easier to get into the Fort Knox vaults than into Morrow, especially now with the angry international controversy about the American and Russian lunar bases going on.

Fairlie unstrapped and went forward, scrambling and slipping, and held onto the back of Kwolek's seat and spoke emphatically into his ear. "Listen, there's been a mix-up somewhere. I'm Professor Robert Fairlie of Massachusetts University, Department of Linguistics. I have no business at Morrow, and I don't want to go any farther with this error that someone has made."

Kwolek shook his head. "No error. Please strap in again, Mr. Fairlie."

"But use your common sense, man!" said Fairlie. "They wouldn't want a linguist at Morrow."

Kwolek shrugged. "I've got my orders. Pick up passenger Robert Fairlie at Washington and bring him to Morrow fast. You see? No error at all."

2

THE R-404 hounded through the night in pursuit of yesterday's daylight. There was darkness beneath with infrequent lights, and dark skies above with scattered stars, and the plane could not quite outrace the turning earth so it could not catch the daylight. But it tried.

Fairlie sat cramped in his bucket-seat and worried. His rump ached, and the belt chafed his middle, and he was cold. "Why in the world would they want me out there? It doesn't make sense!"

The study of language was a science. To Fairlie, it was a thrilling one, the delving into man's known and forgotten tongues, the shape of human speech and thought for ages. But what could it have to do with Morrow?

He puzzled over it, trying to remember all that he could about the whole lunar project. He found that he didn't remember much, it was too far out of his field. Like most people he'd been startled when the first Sputnik went up, back in 1957. The newspaper headlines had kept one informed of the race for space, the American Atlas rocket of 1958, the Russian New Year's moonshot that missed, the first manned satellite flights, and finally the first landings on the Moon.

Russian and American parties had made it almost simultaneously. Now the Soviets had two bases, one in Kepler crater and one in Encke crater, and the Americans had one base, in Gassendi crater. It had been, of course, a tremendous sensation at first. But

13

just as had been the case with atomic energy, the wonder of it had soon faded out in a dull and dreary mess of charges and counter-charges. There had been a Neutralization Agreement in which all nations promised not to use the Moon for military purposes. And the Soviets were filling the UN with charges that the United States was fortifying Gassendi as a missile base. If they weren't, why wouldn't the Americans allow qualified observers to inspect Gassendi? If warmongering capitalist powers tried to carry their plots to the Moon. . . .

That was about all Fairlie could remember, the colorful stories of the first landings and the wrangle about Gassendi that had been going on ever since. He had not been too greatly interested. He had always believed, like the chap in Scott Fitzgerald's novel, that life was best seen through the single window of your own special interest and that the most limited of persons was the all-round man.

He flushed a little when he remembered how he had said that at a discussion of the landings and what old Hodgkins of Psychology had said to him in answer.

"You know what, Fairlie? You're not interested in anything outside philology because you're afraid. You retreat into your nook of scholarly research because you dislike and fear the real world, real people."

Fairlie had resented that. He wasn't a scholarly prig, just because he liked his work and was absorbed in it. He just didn't have time to devote to every sensation that came along. But he wished now that he had learned a little more about this lunar business. It might give him some clue as to why they had sent a fast jet to bring him to Morrow.

He looked at his watch. No need to wonder about it. He would soon find out.

Time passed. And finally Kwolek turned his head and nodded, his lips forming a word.

Morrow.

The door to the Moon, the gateway into space. From here men

14

stepped off into the cold black vacuum to take supplies out to Gassendi. Fairlie craned forward to see.

The jet tilted and turned and then through the cockpit transparency he saw a pattern of lights in the darkness below, rushing past and falling behind them. The lights clotted and clustered more brightly around long barny metal buildings that looked like airplane hangars, and then a tall control tower with many-colored lamps on it flashed by them.

Darkness again, then far ahead a glimpse of a skeletonal tower, a looming scaffolding of girders and behind it, touching it, the sheer shining curve of something tall and arrogant and awesome. That too dropped back out of sight and as Kwolek swung the jet down on a sharper turn, Fairlie saw two other distant glittering towers far, far, in the darkness. Of a sudden he realized that they were rockets and their gantries.

He felt an unexpected electric thrill of excitement. It was one thing to read newspaper stories about the lunar project, to watch telenews pictures of rockets blasting off, to discuss seriously the political implications of the space age. But to swoop out of darkness and glimpse the majesty of the rockets themselves, poised for their leap into infinity, to see the shining shapes that had perhaps been out there and back and had the scars of another world still upon their sides, that was another thing completely.

When the jet touched ground and he finally climbed down out of it, Fairlie turned to look back. But the towering rockets had receded miles away in those few moments and were now only distantly visible. Closer to him were the barny structures and their lights. Closer still was a small cluster of lights around several low, flat buildings.

The air was surprisingly light, dry and warm, so sharply different from a March night in Boston or Washington that it recalled Fairlie to the strangeness of being here at all.

Fairlie turned to Kwolek. "Now what?"

Kwolek nodded toward the headlights of a car that was coming toward them. "Now it's up to them. All I have to do is deliver you here."

15

The headlights were those of a jeep that pulled up beside them. A civilian, a blond, alert young man, got down from it and said "Okay" to Kwolek. Then to Fairlie he said, "Hello, Mr. Fairlie, my name's Hill. I'll take you on in."

"I'd like," Fairlie began stiffly, "some explanation of why—"

"Of course, they'll explain everything," Hill broke in soothingly. "My job is just to check you in. Get in, please."

As the jeep took them away from the plane, Fairlie asked, "Check me in?"

"Security, you know," said Hill. "But since Withers checked you at the other end, it's only routine."

Fairlie, clinging to the edge of the seat as the jeep bounced over the field, felt a little shock. "Then Withers was a Security man? But I thought—" Withers had said that he represented the Smithsonian. Then that was a big fat lie? But why would the Smithsonian lend itself to such a thing?

The New Mexican landscape looked dark and lonesome under the stars, the lights scattered out ahead of them and beyond in the distance the blur of low, dark hills. They were heading, not toward the barny buildings or the far-off rockets, but toward the flat structures.

"Administration," said Hill, nodding ahead.

He stopped the jeep in front of a long, low stuccoed building with a veranda in front.

"This is a building for special personnel," he told Fairlie. "Now if you'll just come along with me."

He opened a door and light poured out. Fairlie walked inside and then stopped. He had expected some kind of an office. This was a not-too-large and rather ratty-looking lounge room. There were three men talking in one corner of it and they turned as Fairlie entered.

"Please wait—they'll be over from Administration in just a little while," said Hill, behind him.

The door closed, and Fairlie turned around but Hill was gone. He turned back as his name was spoken.

"Bob Fairlie. I'll be damned, they got you in on this too?"

16

One of the three men in the lounge was coming toward him. Fairlie knew him at once. Jim Speer. Doctor James Speer of Pacific University, Department of Linguistics. They were good friends although they saw each other infrequently. Speer was fortyish, stocky and plumper than Fairlie remembered him. "Fatter" was the right word. His round pink face was creased with lines of surprise.

"Got me in on what?" Fairlie said, as he shook hands. "What's this all about, Jim?"

Speer laughed. "What a question. I've been asking it for six hours now, since I got here. So have Bogan and Lisetti since *they* got here. But wait, do you know them?"

Fairlie felt a shock. He recognized the other two men now. He had watched them and listened to them at more than one philological convention. They were big men, in his field. The biggest.

Doctor John Bogan was the dean of American philologists, and he knew it. A massive old man with a saturnine face and a great mane of white hair, he had all the arrogance of a "grand old man" of anything. He merely grunted at Fairlie.

But Lisetti was a different type. He was a famous linguist who looked like the polished villain of an old stage melodrama. He was over fifty but his dapper black hair and mustache made him look younger, and he almost hissed in theatrical fashion as he asked Fairlie, "What did they tell you—I mean, to get you here?"

Fairlie, still bewildered, told about the Smithsonian.

"Ha!" said Lisetti. "We all got a fairy story like that. Important research problem, need you at once—and then we find them bringing us here to Morrow. And nobody tells us why. Now why would they want four linguists at Morrow?"

"*I* still say it's a code," said Speer.

Fairlie looked at him. "A code?"

"It stands to reason," said Speer. "There's a big tiff going on between us and the Russians over Gassendi. All those charges. They'd want to know what instructions the Russians are sending

17

out to their lunar bases. Ten to one, we've been brought here to crack a Russian code."

The rumbling voice of Bogan interrupted them. "Three hours. And not a word from anybody. I shall have something to say about this high-handed—"

Bogan, in turn, was interrupted by the opening of the door. Hill came back in and said hastily, "Gentlemen, let me introduce—"

But the foremost of the two men behind Hill shouldered past him, saying, "That's all right, Hill, I'll take it from here."

Hill went out and shut the door, fast, as though he was glad to get out of there.

The man who had spoken to him told them genially, "I'm Nils Christensen, the chief of Lunar Project. This is Glenn DeWitt, formerly of the Air Force, now my assistant in charge of Special Research."

Christensen's face was perfectly familiar to Fairlie, as it had been to everyone since he had been taken out of his place at the head of a great electronics corporation to become the czar of Lunar Project. A slightly idealized portrait of him had twice adorned the cover of Time Magazine. But Fairlie hadn't expected the man to be so big. He was well over six feet and looked like a ruddy, cheerful Viking, but a Viking who wore glasses and who was getting just a little gray at the edges.

DeWitt, the other man, was younger, and beside Christensen he was rather ordinary-looking, a chunky, dark man of forty with a tight face. Suddenly Fairlie remembered that face too, it had been in the newspapers a few years ago. Colonel DeWitt, who had angrily resigned from the Air Force to protest its slowness in developing space-missiles, or something . . .

Christensen shook hands with each of them, repeating their names, and then said, "Please sit down. You are entitled to an explanation, and I'll give it to you fast."

Bogan began a premonitory rumble, but Christensen went on quickly. "To get right down to it, you know the row the Soviets

18

are making over Gassendi, their charges that we have a military missile-base up there?"

They nodded, all except Bogan. Christensen said, "Maybe you've wondered why we simply don't let a Soviet inspection-team look at Gassendi, to disprove the charges?"

Lisetti answered him. "I have wondered. Everybody has wondered."

Christensen said, "Well, I'll tell you why we haven't. We haven't because we can't. There *is* a military base in Gassendi."

The information was stunning. Speer was the first to speak, and he said incredulously, "You mean—we've broken the Neutralization Agreement, and built a missile-base there?"

Christensen shook his head. "I didn't say that. I said there is a military base, or what's left of it, in Gassendi. But we didn't build it. It was there before either the Americans or the Russians reached the Moon. We just found it."

They stared. Lisetti asked, "But who—how long ago?"

"How long was it there before we got there?" Christensen paused. "As nearly as we can estimate, it's been there for around thirty thousand years."

3

HE WAS FALLING fast, very fast, toward the surface of the Moon. It revolved rapidly underneath him in a blur of dark maria and craters and mountain-ranges, but with every revolution of the scene it was closer.

The illusion was so perfect that Fairlie forgot he was watching a screen and hunched forward tensely in his chair. In the darkened room there was no sound except the clicking of the little projector, until Christensen spoke up from beside them.

"That's it, right on the eastern edge of Mare Humorum. See it?"

"The big oval-shaped crater?"

"It's not a crater—it's a mountain-walled plain, strictly speaking. Yes, that's it. Gassendi."

And the vast misshapen oval rushed up toward their eyes, on the screen. No films from this close had been released to the public, and it was fascinating to see this first American landing as the men in the rocket had seen it.

The plunge slowed, and the scene revolved less rapidly. Now to Fairlie's eyes the great crater—he could not think of it as anything else—leaped clear. Most of it was in shadow, for this was the lunar dawn, but the fierce, stark peaks of ragged rock that walled it caught the sunlight and blazed. Great valleys, wells of inky shadow, ran back into the ramparts south and west.

"When our first probe-satellite orbited the Moon," Christensen was saying, "it had a better metals-radiolocator in it than the Russian probe had. Either that, or we were lucky. It spotted metal deposits in Gassendi, and that's why our first landing was there."

Abruptly the screen went dark.

"This next is two days after landing," said Christensen.

The view was a steady one this time, from the floor of the crater. Fairlie saw a bulging dome in the foreground—Dome One of the base—and beyond it the mountains like bright fangs against a black sky of brilliant stars. Men in vac-suits and helmets were running clumsily back toward the dome.

Almost as soon as he took in the scene, it was gone. The next scene was wholly different.

"That was when the first survey party came back," said Christensen. "With the first news of the find. This is twenty-four hours later."

The viewpoint now was from the mouth of one of the valleys that ran back into the mountain rampart. It was brightly illuminated for the sun had lifted above the crater wall behind them and its rays searched the valley. It was more like a great chasm than a valley, and it seemed to run right into the solid cliff and stop there.

Then Fairlie made out a huge opening in the cliff, and something odd about it. "That opening," he said.

But Christensen's voice interrupted. "Wait. This next view is closer."

It was closer, indeed. Fairlie stared with unbelief.

Where the chasm met the cliff there was a gigantic hole or doorway into the rock beyond. Estimating by the comparative size of the vac-suited figures near it, it was at least fifty yards high. It was, or had been, of the shape of a circle with a flattened base, but great forces had been at work here and it was riven and torn. From one side of it hung a vast, buckled slab of dully gleaming metal. Another flat metal mass, that looked as though it had been partly melted, lay sprawled half inside the opening, amid a litter of broken rock and detritus.

"Doors," said Christensen quietly. "Or they were, once. There's

21

a big cavernous space inside the cliff, and there were sliding doors to close it—two sets of them, a giant airlock, in fact."

The projector had stopped on that scene. Now it started whirring again. Christensen said simply, "This is inside."

Floodlights vaguely illuminated a bewildering scene. It had been, once, the symmetrically shaped interior of a vast hollow in the cliff. But it too had been riven and wrecked. There were great splits and gouges in the smooth rock walls, and tumbled masses of broken stone on the floor, and in the foreground amid the rock fragments were gleams of twisted metal plates and girders. Men stood looking at these, their helmets glittering in the light.

"Last, a close-up," said Christensen. "These things were in the wreckage."

This final scene was an anticlimax. It was a close view of two objects—one of them an ordinary-looking metal chair whose standard was badly bent, the other a rod that looked like the broken-off end of a lever, with a grooved grip at its end.

The switches snapped, the lights came on, and DeWitt turned off the small projector he had been operating. They looked at Christensen, and for once even Lisetti was dumb.

"You understand," Christensen said, "these are just a little bit of the filmed material we have. We put these bits together to give you a quick idea of the thing, first."

"And that—all that—has been there in Gassendi for thirty thousand years?" Speer said, finally.

"Yes."

There was a silence, and Fairlie tried to take it in, and could not. Not all of it, not all at once. The mind balked at it. He wondered how the men who had first found this thing had felt. How would Columbus have felt if he had landed in the New World and had found there the ruins of an air-base?

We were all too sure, he thought numbly. Too sure of our knowledge, of our plans. We thought we would know every step of the way we would go. The Moon was to be the first step, the lifeless sphere where we would set up our bases, and then the planets one by one, and for the first time space would be conquered, to the glory of us, forever, amen. And who was to dream that that conquest had been achieved by others long ago? Nobody in the world even *yet* dreamed such a thing, except a handful of men here in Morrow and up in Gassendi. And the secret they guarded was a bomb that would blow human complacency and pride to rags, when it got out.

Fairlie said, "How can they know it's been so long? I mean—I've read that since there's no air or weather on the Moon, nothing changes."

DeWitt answered that, speaking in a flat voice. "Solar and cosmic radiation has measurable effects on metals. The time since the cavern in Gassendi was shattered can be approximated that way."

"But for God's sake," said Lisetti, "why hasn't there been a peep about this? To hide such a discovery—"

Christensen nodded unhappily. "We all feel that way about it. But this is a security matter. *Military* security."

They stared at him. Then after a moment, Speer asked, "You said, 'since the cavern in Gassendi was shattered.' What shattered it?"

"Enemy action. The place was a carefully hidden military base, that's for sure. A military base presupposes enemies. And our experts are quite certain that a weapon or weapons of unknown power and nature, striking from above, hit and wrecked that base of the Ur-men."

"The—what?"

"Ur-men. You know, the German prefix meaning an unknown early type of anything. Like the Ur-Hamlet, and so on. It's the provisional name we've given to the builders of that base."

Lisetti said rapidly, "It's not the 'Ur' I'm questioning—it's the 'men.' "

Christensen looked at him. "You saw that chair and that control-lever?"

"Yes, but what do they—" Lisetti stopped. "I see now. That chair was for a human or near-human to sit in."

"That's right. And the lever-grip was grooved for four fingers.

23

And there have been a lot of other things taken out of the wrecked ships in that cavern base which make it quite certain they were built and used by people of near-human type."

There was a little silence. DeWitt was taking the film out of the projector, carefully putting it into a can which he locked. Christensen got up, as though too restless to sit longer.

"Let me put it this way," he said to them. "There was a war going on, back in that far past. Between the Ur-men, and an enemy or enemies unknown. Both sides had conquered space—interstellar space, we think, and not just interplanetary—and both had weapons of great power. You see how important, militarily, the smashed-up things and ships in that base can be?"

They saw it. Christensen went on, "Because this has to be absolute top-secret, you couldn't be told about it until you were here, inside our Security set-up."

"May I ask just *why* we are here?" rumbled Bogan.

Christensen shrugged. "I thought maybe you'd have guessed by now why a team of linguists would be pulled into this. Give me those pictures, Glenn."

DeWitt took some glossy photographs out of a briefcase and handed them over. Christensen held one for them to see. It was, Fairlie saw, a greatly enlarged photograph of a small oblong plaque attached to an unidentifiable metal surface.

There was a neatly engraved legend on the plaque. It looked at first sight like wildly distorted Arabic printing, and then it didn't appear so much like it, and then it looked like no writing that Fairlie had ever seen before. A thrill shot through him.

"Their writing?"

Christensen nodded. "That's a plaque attached to a machine in the Gassendi ruins. Glenn's men—he's in charge of analyzing these things—say it was a kind of oxygenator. That's Ur-man writing. We have other such samples, and a lot of records they left when they abandoned the ruined base. We want them deciphered."

The enormity of the suggestion struck them all dumb except

24

for Bogan. He got majestically to his feet, and instead of roaring he spoke to Christensen with a kind of gentle contempt.

"You don't know much about linguistics, do you?"

"Not much," Christensen said cheerfully. "But the four of you have all done noteworthy things in puzzling out ancient languages. We hope you can do it again."

Bogan gave him a look that had for a generation set graduate students cringing.

"Decipher an unknown language with no referents whatever, no possible bilingual comparisons?" he exclaimed.

Christensen nodded. "That's right. It'll probably be tough. But it was tough getting to Gassendi at all. I'm sure you'll work it out."

Bogan was too outraged for immediate rejoinder to that, and Christensen hurried on before he could be interrupted. "Besides, you won't be completely without referents. The nature, purpose and design of the machines can surely point to the meaning of the inscriptions on them. Glenn will cooperate with you on that."

DeWitt silently nodded.

Christensen went to the door, turned there, and said, "You're drafted, gentlemen. For a job affecting national security in the most vital way. I know you'll do your best and will comply with all Security regulations. Good night." He went on out.

DeWitt put the photographs back into the briefcase, picked up the can of film, and told them, "I'll start going over this stuff with you tomorrow. Hill will show you your quarters and all that."

And he too went out.

The four looked at each other, and Fairlie wondered if his face was as ridiculous in its expression as Lisetti's and Speer's were. They three were like men who had been tossed suddenly into icy cold water and could not get their breath.

Not Bogan. He began to give his opinion of Christensen, of the effrontery of it all, in a flow of the measured, biting phrases for which he was famous. "A manufacturer, an industrialist, telling scholars what they can and can't do!"

They did not have much interest in Bogan's resentment, they were too staggered yet. Fairlie was glad when Hill came in.

25

"I'll take you to your quarters. In the morning I'll show you the office and other facilities we have for you."

They went out into the windy darkness. Irregular patterns of lights defined the near and distant buildings. It was quiet except for the sound of a truck pulling out of a car-pool off to the left. The wind had a gritty feel to it, bringing sand and dust from the dark flatness around them.

Fairlie looked up at the sky as he followed Hill. Orion strode mightily toward the zenith, followed by the upward-leaping stars of Canis Major, and all the heavens were sown with constellations that wavered wind-bright. He remembered what Christensen had said, that both long-ago enemies had conquered interstellar space, not just interplanetary.

Remembering, it seemed suddenly to Fairlie that the quiet of the starry sky was strange, like the quiet of a deserted battlefield.

4

A MAN'S STRONG voice spoke out of the depths of space and time. The words were unfamiliar and meaningless, but the voice itself had meaning. There were authority and pride in it, and a strength that made the resonant phrases rolling out of the loudspeaker echo from the walls of the little laboratory.

DeWitt sat hunched forward, listening, his eyes almost shut and his fingers clenching hungrily with the rhythm of that alien speech, as though he would reach out and tear meaning bodily from the sounds. Fairlie understood how DeWitt felt. What was he speaking of, this man who had lived and died ages ago? Was this the record of some nightmare shock of conflict in the unimaginable war that had once stormed through the suns? Was he telling of triumph, or of defeat?

This was neither the first nor the only time Fairlie had listened to that same voice, but it was impossible to retain the proper scholarly detachment. The blood beat faster, the nerves of the scalp crept and tingled, the palms of the hands were wet. This was a man speaking to other men in the moment of some overwhelming crisis, and every word was charged with importance and a curious immediacy. Curious because the immediacy of thirty thousand years ago could hardly have much effect on a present-day listener—and yet it did.

For some time a most uncomfortable and scientifically reprehensible conviction had been growing in Fairlie that the message he

27

was listening to was as vital to him as it had been for the people to whom it was first spoken, and that he must understand it before it was too late.

Must understand it. And the voice rolled on, and the shapes and forms of speech became almost recognizable, and just beyond, just over the threshold, understanding lurked in the darkness waiting, waiting for the one Word of Power to coax it forth.

Illusion. And the voice stopped, and there was nothing.

DeWitt looked at Fairlie as though he hated him. But Fairlie knew that the hatred was not personal. It was the frustration that DeWitt hated, and Fairlie was only the symbol of it.

"Do you want another one?" DeWitt asked.

Fairlie shook his head. "This is enough for today." He switched off the tape-recorder.

DeWitt rose. He shut off the amplifier and then bent over the square plastic box to which the amplifier was connected. Inside the transparent plastic a two-inch silvery ball was fixed upon a plastic pin. The ball had been turning very slowly. Now as DeWitt watched it the rotation slowed still more and then stopped, and there was the tiniest of audible clicks. DeWitt sighed. With the tenderness of a mother lifting her first-born he cupped his fingers around the metal sphere and removed it from the pin.

Fairlie said, "I still don't understand how so much speech is recorded on that little ball of metal."

"We don't know either," DeWitt said bitterly. He placed the ball in a rack which contained dozens of similar balls, carefully nested. "We got it to working, but that's all. Theoretically the recording device, instead of making sounds form patterns of iron particles on tape, formed patterns of atoms instead, perhaps even electrons. An invisible beam scans them to reproduce the sound-waves, but we haven't even been able to find out exactly what kind of a beam."

He looked at the rack and the rows of bright little enigmas sitting hard and unconcerned in the harsh laboratory light.

"All that knowledge there," he said. "We've got it right in our hands. Their own voices, their own words, right there, all of it, and it's—" He made an abrupt violent gesture with his hands and turned away from the rack. "How are you coming, Fairlie? Haven't you made any progress at all?"

"Mr. DeWitt," said Fairlie. "With what politeness I have been able to muster I've asked you please to quit riding me." He turned on the recorder and punched the rewind. The brown tape went hissing back off the take-up reel and he watched it gloomily.

"Do you have any idea how long it takes to translate a forgotten language even when you *have* bilingual inscriptions, a Rosetta Stone? Decades. Generations. And in this case—" Fairlie slammed the STOP and the tape was still, quiet and uncommunicative as the silvery balls in the rack.

"We haven't got decades," said DeWitt softly. "We haven't got years. We're lucky if we have months."

Fairlie looked at him.

"Too much pressure," DeWitt said. "One of these days Gassendi will blow wide open, it has to. The UN will force an investigation. After that—it belongs to everybody. If we don't make use of the time we have before that happens, we'll be as dead and lost as the Ur-men. We've got to have this knowledge, and we've got to have it first."

"Then how about getting out of here and letting me work?" said Fairlie irritably. He wavered between admiration of DeWitt's competence and intense dislike of his driving impatience with other people's problems. He seemed to think that a job like this was no different from weaving baskets or hoeing turnips and that all you had to do to speed it up was simply to work harder.

Without waiting for any answer from DeWitt he jacked in the connection between the tape-recorder and the sonograph, turned them both on, and set the recorder control for playback.

Once more the deep strong voice spoke out across the gulf of thirty millennia, and once more the nerves tightened in the pit of Fairlie's stomach and the spur of need was on him. He resolutely ignored that for what it was—sheer emotional nonsense—and concentrated on the revolving drum of the sonograph, where a phosphor needle was busy constructing on the sensitive paper a

29

graph based on analysis of the sounds played back from the tape and passed through the heart of the sonograph, a battery of tiny radio tubes tuned to successive frequencies.

DeWitt had not gone. He was listening again, listening and peering at the building graph with that hungry-hawk look— rip and tear and pull it out, no nonsense, *make* it go the way it should go, damn it!

"Why are some parts of the graph so much blacker than others?" he asked.

"Degree of blackness indicates comparative intensity of sound."

DeWitt grunted. "All right. So you make a picture of the sound. Why is that easier to understand than the spoken words?"

In a tone that implied the answer to that ought to be apparent to a five-year-old child, Fairlie explained, "A sound is fleeting. It comes and goes. You can't hold it still to study it, and compare it with other sounds. As a visible graph you can do that. And the first step in studying any spoken language is analysis to determine the number of its basic phonemes, the smallest units of speech-sound."

"Sounds simple enough."

"Try it. And after you have the phonemes, then there are the morphemes and the positional variants and—"

"Fairlie."

"What?"

"I was in Gassendi."

The voice from the tape-recorder sounded its call to arms— or to flight? Or to the last-ditch desperate courage of men who no longer have any choice about dying but only about the manner in which they will do it?

DeWitt watched the complex graph building under the needle and said, "I was one of the first to see it. I can't tell you what that was like. I won't even try. But I walked past those broken doors and into that cavern, and I looked for bodies in the ruins, expecting every minute to see— But there weren't any. The survivors took care of all their dead and injured. They couldn't have had much time, but they made time for that."

30

And what epic of heroism and endurance was implicit in those words, thought Fairlie.

"One other thing they did was to remove any machines that had escaped damage when the base was shattered. Nothing was left that an enemy might turn to his own use—then."

"But now?" asked Fairlie, knowing that it was expected of him.

"Now an enemy—our enemy—could learn a whole new technology from the wreckage in that base, the machines, the generators, the ships—starships, Fairlie, not just little rockets that have all they can do to jump across the tiny crack that separates us from the Moon. I just want you to think about that, turn it over in your mind, picture a fleet of ships with somebody else's flag on them, a hostile flag, heading out from Earth. Out from Earth, out from the Solar System, clear out—"

His hand made a curving gesture in the air and something about it, coupled with the strange look that had come into DeWitt's eyes and the odd quiet tone of his voice, hit Fairlie with a tremendous impact. For a second the prosaic laboratory was gone and he *saw* the ships, the vast dark mighty shadows against the stars, heading out . . .

"Out," he asked, "to where?"

In that same remote and quiet voice DeWitt answered, "It must have occurred to you that the Ur-men came to our Solar System from somewhere."

Fairlie reached out and stopped the tape-recorder. The needle hung motionless over the graph.

"Oh, no," Fairlie said. He laughed. "But of course that's impossible. Not their coming, I mean, but our going—anybody going—that far. Not now, at least. Not for many years."

DeWitt turned to Fairlie and smiled. "That depends on you."

He turned away and Fairlie watched him walk across the narrow room to the rack and take from it one of the silvery balls. It was a very odd moment, like the moments in a fever-dream when time and space are both distorted and people move about in a manner quite different from their normal habit and the light is queer. There was a great deal that Fairlie wanted to

31

say but he couldn't find the means to say it. And all the time DeWitt was fixing the tiny ball on the pin and operating the mysterious controls.

When Fairlie did finally speak it was an explosive inanity. "I told you I didn't want any more tapes this time."

The voice of a fretful child. And the ships would go out, and it was up to him—

Up to him.

DeWitt's voice was perfectly casual when he answered. "This isn't a message recording. Purely an entertainment piece. They left behind a lot of non-essential stuff like that—probably the most important records went with them. I just thought you might like to hear this. Give you a little different slant on the Ur-men, their aesthetic rather than their warlike and/or mechanical side."

The tiny ball began to turn on its slender pin.

A sound came into the laboratory, the feather-edge of a clear wind blowing across the stars. It came out of infinity, very sweet and distant, and you could hear it coming closer and it was almost more than you could bear, this clear whistling soaring and falling with such joyous purity, and what kind of an instrument made it, anyway—an organ-pipe, a flute, a harp? No, none of these. Something strange, something never played on Earth, and yet there were echoes. The tears sprang to his eyes and the sound swooped down the whole long curve of the galaxy in a beautiful descending trill and then passed on, receding into the infinity from which it came.

Before it was quite lost, the woman began to sing.

5

SHE CALLED TO the wandering star-wind and it answered her from far off. She called again and it came to her with a leap and a trill clear back across the galaxy, and Fairlie thought that anything, even a wind, would come to the calling of that voice.

It was round and full, produced with such ease that the tone was like warm silver, never pinched or strained, never shrill. The voice and the wind began to talk to each other—without words, but there was no need of words. The pattern of sound was simple, almost antique, but indescribably beautiful. Then the call-and-response became more complex and before the listening ear was aware of the change other voices had joined in, on the side of the wind—instrumental voices of such strangeness that Fairlie could not even guess how the sounds they made were produced.

They were rather shattering at first, but the woman's voice welcomed them as old friends, singing now with them, now against them, and after a minute or two the strangeness faded and only the eerie beauty of the sounds remained, weaving patterns of increasing complexity around that silvery voice. It dawned on Fairlie, very dimly because he didn't know much about music, that he was listening to a superb and joyous fugue such as Bach might have written if Bach had been a Dorian or an ancient Egyptian, and the instruments for which the music was created something not yet invented in any of the cultures of Earth.

He listened and in his mind's eye he could see the woman—

33

not clearly, but he knew that she was beautiful—standing on a high place singing and all about her a beat and whirl and flash of wings, now dark, now shining, as the clustered stars swooped down and sang around her.

The silence when it was all over was a shock to Fairlie's ears.

"Effective, isn't it?" DeWitt said, and the ball stopped turning. "Remarkably human voice, too—just like the man's. Their vocal equipment couldn't have been too different from ours. Well, I still have a session with Speer ahead of me." He commenced deftly to pack up the alien recorder and the rack of silver balls. "Think over what we've been talking about, Fairlie. Call me when you're ready for more tapes. And let me know immediately if you come up with anything."

He was gone before Fairlie could wrench his stupefied brain back into its proper channel. And long after the door closed Fairlie was still thinking about the woman on the mountain-top singing to the stars.

He did not get much work done the rest of that day. He did not sleep very well that night, nor the night after that, and when he did he saw visions of such strangeness that he started up from them wide-awake and sweating. He began to work with a new intensity, harder than he had ever worked in his life before, but there was little joy in it. His shoulders seemed bowed with a great weight and there was an oppressiveness in the very air about him. When he looked at himself in the mirror while he shaved each morning it seemed to him that every day the face he saw looked older and more harried, the eyes more eager and yet more haunted.

He saw very little of the others, and when he did see them he thought that they too were laboring under the same fear, the same urgent hunger as himself. Oddly, in those first weeks, nobody mentioned any of the terrifying implications that DeWitt had brought up to Fairlie and so presumably to the others as well. Fairlie wanted to talk about these things, desperately, but whenever he tried he knew he could not because he had not yet really accepted them himself. Part of his mind was still involved

34

in the struggle to tear down the basic concepts upon which the world and his life in it had always rested, and which had now with such brutal suddenness become inadequate.

The ships will go out. Somebody's ships, theirs or ours. The stars are waiting, and it depends on you.

That was too big a load to share with anybody. A man had to learn to carry it himself before he could even admit it was there.

And time went on.

Fairlie and Speer carried out their phonematic analyses independently. At the same time Bogan and Lisetti also independently, were working on a glossematic analysis of the written Ur-speech, glossemes being the smallest unit of significant meaning just as phonemes were the smallest unit of meaningful sound. There was not, of course, any discussion between them about how their separate jobs were progressing. Fairlie made his graphs and marked out his probable phonemes and checked and compared and did it all over again, knowing all the time that if his findings did not check with Speer's, or if the glossematic analyses failed to show any results, the labor was all for nothing.

There were many times when he thought that that would be a good thing and prayed for it to happen.

There were other times when he was sick with apprehension that the secret of the Ur-men would remain locked away forever in incomprehensible speech and undecipherable writing. The ships would never fly, the stars would glimmer and go out, and there would be nothing for him ever again but dusty visionless classrooms and yawning students.

These were the times when he listened to the singing of the Ur-woman. He did this more and more often, and it was increasingly difficult to make himself understand that the singer had been dead for thirty thousand years. The voice was there, alive and ringing, and it called to him.

He prepared his notes, wrote a careful summary of his findings, and met with Speer. Their findings checked.

Bogan and Lisetti, in the meantime, were comparing their own independently-arrived-at results on the analysis of similarities between the plaques on Ur-machines and those on Earthly machines of similar use. Bogan made it known that he was ready for a general session, and it was held in the middle of a hot bright morning in the shabby lounge. Four men in shirtsleeves with tomorrow in their sweaty hands. DeWitt sat in. He did not say anything, and physically he did nothing but sit in a chair and smoke, but he spread a tension through the room as tangible as a static charge.

Bogan, naturally, spoke first. "Dr. Lisetti and I have achieved almost identical results." The word *almost* deplored Lisetti's unfortunate stupidity. "On the basis of these results we can say with reasonable certainty that certain symbols or combinations of symbols can be translated as ON and OFF, or OPERATIVE and NON-OPERATIVE. Other symbols are identifiable as numerals in a digital system, and we have agreed on a partial listing of their values. We have also agreed on the probable interpretation of several other groups of symbols."

DeWitt said, "Then you've done it."

Bogan looked at him. "Done what?"

"Found the key to the translation." He stood up, leaning forward over the table. "How long will it take you to do it now that you're started?"

"Oh, for God's sake," said Bogan. "Why must one always be burdened with fools?" The cry was one of genuine anguish, and Fairlie realized that these weeks had told on Bogan as much as on any of them. The pompous façade was now only a shell maintained by habit. Behind it was a tired and frightened man no different from the rest of them.

"I suppose," said DeWitt, "because there are so many of us." His eyes were hot. "However, I do happen to know something about cryptography and in the light of that knowledge my question does not seem to me to be idiotic."

Bogan shook his head. "I'm sorry. But we are not dealing with cryptography, where the basic language is known and it is only necessary to determine what substitution of symbology has been made for it. We are confronted with total unknowns."

"You said you had identified certain words and numbers. That should certainly give you a clue."

"I said we had agreed on the probable meanings of certain symbols. That's quite a different thing."

"How so?"

"We still don't know what the symbols *are*. Whether they're pictograms, ideograms, letters of an alphabet, or stylized symbols that are simply that and no more, with an arbitrary meaning— just as a skull-and-crossbones always means POISON when you see it on a bottle. We have *guessed* at the meaning of other symbols because their position and application would seem to be the same as those similarly positioned on our own machines, but these are only guesses as yet and damned dangerous ones to depend on in actually operating the machines."

He ran a distracted hand through his mane of hair and pointed to the stacks of reports on the table.

"The work has only begun. Only barely begun. Not only do we have to determine the nature of the script, we have to determine the nature of the language. Is it agglutinative, syllabic, or—"

"The work *has* begun, though," DeWitt said flatly. "You have made progress."

"To the extent I have just outlined."

"Then I think we should have Christensen down here."

And Christensen came.

The day went on, reaching a crescendo of heat and glare, descending by imperceptible gradations to abrupt twilight and a cooling of the air, and then to night. Food was brought in, and a great deal of coffee, and many packs of cigarettes. About eleven-thirty the talking and thrashing of papers was done. Fairlie sagged in his chair, too tired to care what happened next, one part of his mind grappling like a sleepwalker with the new data that had come into it and already automatically planning out the next step he wanted to take.

The other part of his mind was listening to Christensen's incredibly unwearied voice telling them all what a splendid job they were doing and how he was sure that teamwork like this would eventually solve all the problems confronting them. Goosegrease, Fairlie thought, but pleasant to hear.

Then DeWitt said, "I think it's time to get moving."

Christensen looked at him. "In just what way?"

"Initiate a ship project. With what these gentlemen know now we can make a beginning—start running tests of the actual Ur-machines that we've repaired."

Christensen's face became bland, impenetrable, and hard as stone. "We're all anxious to get started, Glenn, but let's not go off half-cocked. We need to know an awful lot more before we start testing or any projects. Dr. Bogan and Dr. Lisetti have made it quite clear that operational procedures for these machines are still uncertain."

DeWitt smiled. "I know that. But I say it's time we got out of uncertainty and started doing something. Some physical tests—"

"—could easily result in disaster. No. It's far too premature." Christensen got up, a polite signal that the discussion was over.

DeWitt ignored it. "I don't think it is. What are we waiting for? A complete translation of every word? We can't wait that long. And as for the machines, some practical tests would help speed up the work." He turned swiftly to Bogan and the others. "Isn't that so, gentlemen?"

Bogan opened his mouth, but before he could get anything out of it Christensen spoke. "We will not have any tests at this time."

"Then when?" demanded DeWitt.

"When I decide that the work has progressed far enough to make it practicable."

"And I wonder just when that will be, if ever."

Christensen said quietly, "Did you mean something by that?"

"Yes, I did. You know what I think, Chris? I think you're scared of this thing. I think you'll put off the evil day as long as you possibly can." He paused. "Why don't we let Washington decide?"

Fairlie, watching this, saw that Christensen was angry—and Christensen angry was a formidable sight. Fairlie thought that Glenn DeWitt had more courage than he would have to face up

38

to it. He began to understand now the kind of fierce impatience that had made DeWitt leave the Air Force.

After a minute Christensen said in a cool voice, "Very well, Glenn, you go to Washington and take it up with the Defense Secretary himself. I'll send in my own report, and we'll see what the decision is."

"Fine," DeWitt said, and went out. Christensen stood for a moment looking intently at nothing in particular. Bogan harrumphed and began to sweep papers together. He ignored Christensen.

"I suggest that we confer again in four or five weeks to exchange notes on what progress has been made—if any."

Christensen said abruptly, "Keep me informed. Good night, gentlemen."

He went out. The others straggled after him. Outside in the dark night and the wind Fairlie paused to look at the sky with its billion bristling stars, and Speer spoke from behind his shoulder.

"I wish I knew," said Speer, "how this will all turn out."

Fairlie grunted. The wind felt icy on him, stabbing through his clothes to the naked skin underneath. He began to shiver.

"There's something else I wish, too," said Speer in a different voice. "I wish to God they'd left me out of it."

He turned and went away.

Bogan and Lisetti had heard him. They looked at each other and at Fairlie, their faces pale and indistinct, blurred in the starshine.

"Amen," said Lisetti.

"Well, they didn't," said Bogan, "and so we may as well make the best of it. But I may also wish into eternal hellfire the man who roused up the nasty little beast I call conscience. It isn't a creature I've ever cared to wrestle with, and in our field of science one is hardly ever called upon to do it."

Lisetti looked up at the sky. He was shivering too.

"Oh hell," he said. "I am going to bed and get drunk. In that order."

They walked away from each other toward their separate

39

quarters, small lonely figures in the wide dark, and none of them looked up again at the sky above them.

The work started again. The endless analyses, the comparisons, the hopeful trials and wholly expected defeats. In spare moments he wondered how DeWitt was doing in Washington, and swung as usual between hope that the Defense Secretary would listen to Christensen and forbid the tests, and then that he would listen to DeWitt and give them full speed ahead.

A week or so later DeWitt walked in on him and Fairlie didn't have to ask how it had gone. His hard face told very plainly that the official word had been a large round NO.

"We'll never get off the ground now until you people give us more to go on. Is there any hope of that in the foreseeable future?"

Nettled by DeWitt's harsh sarcasm, Fairlie took considerable pleasure in telling him that there was no hope at all.

"And anyway," he added, "I think Christensen's right. It's absurd to try and learn a whole new technology on the basis of two words, OFF and ON."

"Seems to me that's about all you need," DeWitt said softly. "I'm surprised at you, Fairlie, I thought you were a young man, but I see you're as old as Christensen, though you haven't any right to be. I can see why Christensen finds it hard to make the change-over, to look up instead of back. But you—" He shook his head and went out, leaving Fairlie hot with a rage he did not quite understand.

He turned on the recorder and listened to the woman singing, calling across time and the shining of countless stars. He hated Christensen and the Secretary of Defense.

He began to work with a new intensity, almost with frenzy. His lights burned late into the night, and few hours out of the twenty-four were wasted in sleep. He lived largely on black coffee and benzedrine. The world contracted around him until it was only large enough to contain himself, his tapes, his photostats and graphs, his notebooks, and the figurative stone wall against which he beat in an insane sort of way.

And after a certain time a little crack seemed to appear in the

40

wall. He knew that it was not really there because it was based on an impossibility, a line he had followed out of sheer exhausted desperation and dropped as soon as he had had some sleep. Only he kept sneaking back to it because it was the only line that had produced any results at all, even spurious ones.

He did not tell anybody about it, not even Speer. He was ashamed to.

And then one night quite late the lights went out all in the wink of a second.

He stood up in the dark, startled. He had the recorder on and the voice of the Ur-woman filled his ears, but even so he could hear the faint skirling of the wind around the corner, the flick of blown sand against the window-pane. There was nothing else. The line had blown down, he thought, or else there had been a general power failure on the base. He groped his way to the door and stepped out to have a look.

And the distant glitter of lights around Administration were the first and the last things he saw.

6

THE QUESTIONING had been going on for years.

Centuries.

"How did you know the wires had been cut?"

"I didn't, damn it, not then, you told me that yourself."

Hill's face, cold, grim, furious. Hill caught napping, Base Security caught with its guard down. Behind Hill there was Christensen, and DeWitt, looking as though the sky had fallen on them.

"Very well," said Hill, "you didn't know it." His tone implied that Fairlie was telling a clumsy lie but that he, Hill, would pretend to believe it. "Let's go over the whole thing again from the beginning. You heard a sound."

"I did not," said Fairlie, "hear any sound. And I am not going to go over the whole thing again from the beginning." He looked at them all with sullen hatred. The aspirin was beginning to wear off and he could feel his head again. He pointed to it in a fury of exasperation. "Look. I've got a goose-egg on my skull the size of the Matterhorn. Your own Medical Officer has examined it and pronounced it bona fide. I didn't give it to myself. Nor did I steal my own notebooks."

When he thought of the notebooks and all the work that had gone into them his rage mounted.

"The tapes and the photographs that were taken can be replaced, but not my notebooks. And I'll tell you something, Mr. Hill. I ought to be questioning you instead of the other way around. Why weren't you on the job? Why wasn't I given protection?" He glared around at them all. "I didn't ask to come here, you people tricked me into it without even giving me a chance to say no, and now you have the colossal effrontery to—" He choked on the words. "Actually to accuse me of—"

"All right," said Hill wearily, "calm down. If you think you're getting a grilling you should see what's happening to your colleagues. I turned my experts loose on them." He began to walk up and down. "We don't necessarily suspect you, or them. But we've got to find out who—"

"You're too late," DeWitt said bitterly. "I don't care who took the stuff, that's your problem. The point is it was taken. Now *They* know about Gassendi. Now *They* have tapes and pictures and Fairlie's notebooks with a record of all the work done to date."

"More than that," said Fairlie. "I was working on a new approach. I don't really believe I was right, but I was getting some surprising results, and if I *was* right—"

There was a stricken silence.

Christensen said in a chilled-steel voice, "May I ask why you didn't report this to me?"

"Because I wasn't ready to," snapped Fairlie. "I hadn't even mentioned it to Speer. I needed to check it out much more thoroughly."

DeWitt was on his feet and Fairlie thought for a moment that the man was going to throttle him. "You were getting results and you didn't tell us?"

"I wasn't sure!"

"I shouldn't think there'd be any doubt. Either you can translate a language or you can't."

"Did you ever hear of ancient Sumerian? It's a lovely agglutinative language and there was quite a lot of it left around on clay tablets. It was translated. And after some of those first translations had been acclaimed and widely published, it was discovered that this lovely language could be translated in several other ways equally as well and that much of what had been pub-

43

lished was just flatly wrong." He scowled at DeWitt and then turned away.

"Anyway, the premise I was going on was basically absurd and I knew it. It was just that I *seemed* to be getting somewhere—an easy trap to fall into—and I couldn't resist playing with it."

"What was the premise?" asked DeWitt almost gently.

"It struck me one night that the Ur-language bore a superficial structural resemblance to this language I was just talking about—Sumerian. I started to doodle around with the idea in my spare time, meaning when I was up against another stone wall and couldn't think of anything else to do. The Ur-folk, whoever they were, certainly didn't speak Sumerian or anything like it. It just isn't in the bounds of reason that the language of another star should bear any real resemblance to any tongue of Earth. And yet the crazy part of it was, it worked. Or it seemed to."

"Well," said DeWitt. "That just about wraps it up. If Fairlie was on the right track—" He turned furiously on Christensen. "You see what all this paltering and delay has done? This was bound to happen sooner or later. They were *bound* to find out what we're doing in Gassendi, and now we're licked, we're really licked. In a few days they'll know as much or more about it than we do. And they won't have to wait while a succession of cautious grandmothers decide whether it's safe to do something. They'll just build a ship and go."

DeWitt paused. "We've lost the stars, Chris. We had them, right here." He held out his hand. "And we've lost them. And they're the smallest thing we've lost. Begin with our freedom and our peace of mind and go on from there."

"Rendell's on his way here now from Washington," Christensen said. "I notified him immediately, of course."

"That's wonderful," snarled DeWitt. "I'm sure the change of air will do the Secretary good, but what else he'll accomplish I don't know." He picked up his hat. "The hell with it. We had our chance. Now we're through." He went out, slamming the door smartly behind him.

Christensen shook his head. "I doubt if the outlook is as bad

44

as all that," he said. But he looked worried. "Hill, is there any chance that material has not been taken from the Base yet?"

Hill said, "You asked me that before."

"I'm asking you again."

"And my answer is the same. Namely, I don't know but I strongly doubt it. During the time that elapsed between the attack on Fairlie and our notification of it the spy had ample opportunity to get the stuff out if he had carefully planned in advance just how to do it, and I can't imagine he didn't. Security is just about as tight at Morrow as it's humanly possible to make it, but—" He shrugged. He was not a happy man.

"Humanly possible." Christensen nodded. "And nothing human is ever perfect. Just the same, Hill, I want that spy."

"You'll get him."

Christensen rounded on Fairlie. "Go back to your quarters and hold yourself in readiness. As soon as I've seen the Secretary, and as soon as Hill's men are through with your colleagues, I want a meeting. You'd better jot down anything you can remember from your notes."

"But—" said Fairlie, thinking of the immense scorn that would be heaped upon him, and rightly, by Bogan and the others.

He was talking to Christensen's back. The back vanished through the door. Fairlie shut his jaw with a snap and glanced at Hill.

"You," said Hill, "think you have worries." He sat down at the desk and began punching buttons.

Fairlie went back to his quarters.

They had been systematically searched. Some items were missing—chiefly his correspondence, letters from his mother, and a small file of articles from scholarly journals that he had thought might be useful. He supposed they were going to test them for codes and invisible writing. They had not replaced his socks and underwear in their proper order. It irritated him to have things out of place and he did a hasty clean-up and cursed as he did it, because he was angry at having his belongings tampered with.

Then he took more aspirin, got out a fresh notebook and began an agonized experiment in total recall.

It was by no means total, but it was more than enough, as he had foreseen, to call down the wrath of Bogan and Lisetti upon him when they met the next day, with Christensen and DeWitt sitting in. Even Speer looked disgusted. None of them were in a good frame of mind anyway, after long hours of examination by Hill's men.

Fairlie endured their comments patiently. "I'm not defending this approach," he said. "Matter of fact, I thoroughly agree with you. Bringing it up at this time was not my idea. I am merely complying with Mr. Christensen's orders."

Bogan said sourly, "You shouldn't have brought it up to him in the first place."

"Perhaps not. But there was just that little nagging one-in-a-million chance. Suppose I hadn't mentioned it, only to find out later on that I should have."

"Fairlie's fault was in not mentioning it sooner," DeWitt said. "We might have had something definite to take to Rendell weeks ago."

"Impossible," said Bogan flatly.

"Let me ask you this," Christensen said. "Have you made any progress along the other lines you've been pursuing?"

They hated to say it because it was obvious what the next step would be. Fairlie watched them trying to get around it but there wasn't any way. The answer was No.

"Then I suggest you try Fairlie's approach whether you believe in it or not. If it proves worthless, well and good. We'll drop it. But I want it proved, not merely assumed."

He stood up, a very formidable man with a terrible burden on his shoulders, and for once even Bogan was not disposed to quarrel with him.

"Secretary of Defense Rendell has flown back to Washington to meet with the Security Council and discuss the immediate launching of a project. He feels, and I feel——" here Christensen looked at DeWitt—"that we still have a small lead in time and that

46

there is still a chance if we expend every possible effort. Those who stole the records will certainly check out Fairlie's results in translating the Ur-language. I don't believe I have to explain how vital it is for us to do the same, and without any prejudice. We can't afford our cherished separate identity as scholars any more, gentlemen. We've shrunk right down with the rest of the free world. I'm afraid it's now a simple matter of survival."

DeWitt said darkly, "I doubt if we have a chance even so. But if there is one, you'd better get busy."

7

It was several weeks later, and Fairlie stood in an unfamiliar place awaiting a double test.

The place was a concrete bunker sunk in the floor of a rocky gorge in the test area of Morrow Base. It was crammed with control panels and instruments presided over by young men of a brusquely competent sort who spoke a language as remote to Fairlie's understanding as the language of the Ur-folk itself.

More so, now. Because Fairlie thought he could understand at least a part of what the Ur-folk had said and written. That was one half of the test. He and his fellow linguists, using his methods, had arrived at identical and reasonably clear translations of the plaques on the mechanisms DeWitt was most interested in—the ion-drive generators.

At separate points in the walls of barren and blistering rock that were visible through the bunker viewports two of these generators, brought from Gassendi, had been anchored into test-stands. In a very few minutes Number One would be fired and Fairlie would know whether his approach to the Ur-language was correct or disastrously wrong.

It was hot in the bunker from the outside sun and the crowding of bodies, but Fairlie felt cold and a little nauseated. He was scared.

The voices of the technicians were crisp and undisturbed. De-Witt was sweating, firing his words in short bursts now at the

48

technicians, now at the big brass of Operation Darkness who stood with Christensen and Fairlie in the close space and waited.

Operation Darkness. There was something ominous about that name, Fairlie thought. He wished they had chosen some other code designation for their project. Starfire, or Future Hope, or Gallant Lunacy, anything a little more cheerful.

Operation Darkness.

In a few minutes they would know whether or not they had the power to get it off the ground.

He looked at the men responsible for the project, trying to guess what they were thinking in these last moments before the test. There were three of them, Raab the physicist, Winstedt the biologist, Thomason the engineer. They had arrived at Morrow hard on the heels of the Security Council's decision to go full speed ahead with the building of a ship. All of them were, or should be, running scared like DeWitt. But it was hard to guess anything from their faces. They were all sweating, but that was the heat.

Raab, dark, thin, and middle-aged, was absorbed in cabalistic discussion with a couple of the technicians. He did not appear to have any emotions. Fairlie thought Raab was the coldest man he had ever met. His mind was like a steel trap with all the surfaces polished to an incredible brilliance. His body appeared to be merely a convenient adjunct, a means of nourishing and transporting the brain, without any particular volitions of its own. It was impossible to imagine Raab as a small boy. It was impossible to imagine him laughing.

Winstedt, on the other hand, did a great deal of laughing, and smiling, and patting of shoulders. Fairlie thought of an expression his grandmother had been fond of using. Smooth as a snake in oil. Winstedt was as much politician as scientist, perhaps more, though his ability as a biologist was unquestioned. He had sleek round cheeks and a sleek round bulge under his belt, and Fairlie would have bet money that Winstedt's interest in the success of Operation Darkness was based firmly on the good it would do Winstedt.

Thomason the engineer was another one like DeWitt, blocky, stocky, hard-driving, tough as beryllium steel, immensely capable, brilliant in one field and illiterate in every other. He was doing a great deal of conferring with DeWitt and with another set of technicians.

Christensen stood quietly in the cramped space and managed somehow to be as withdrawn from the others as though he were a hundred miles away. There was a brooding look about him. Fairlie had watched it grow from the time Operation Darkness became a reality. Perhaps Christensen had, up to that moment, held to the belief that the project could not be activated for a very long time, perhaps never. DeWitt had accused him of deliberate obstructionism and perhaps DeWitt was right.

Fairlie was not at all sure he did not agree with Christensen. And he thought he knew what result Christensen would like to have from the test. Fairlie himself didn't know what he wanted. If the test was successful, then his method of approach was right and he had accomplished a triumph in linguistics second to none. If he was wrong—well, then, he was wrong, and the Project would be delayed, more or less indefinitely.

Maybe even permanently? And whatever happened he would not have any gnawing pangs of conscience, having tried honestly and honestly failed.

And perhaps everybody in the world would be saved a great deal of trouble.

"We're ready," said DeWitt.

Last-second checks of instruments, a movement toward the viewports. Somebody began a countdown. Fairlie squinted his eyes against the harsh glaring of sun on tawny rock. The gorge looked like the Abomination of Desolation, a suitable crucible for the testing of apocalyptic fires. A very cold tentacle closed around Fairlie's insides and coiled tight.

"Fire."

Fairlie visualized the leaping impulse racing faster than thought through remote-control relays. He braced himself.

Nothing happened.

50

Thomason and Raab were glued to their indicator panels.

"I'm getting some kind of a reaction," Raab said. "But very slight."

Thomason said, "There's no perceptible thrust developing." He turned and glowered at DeWitt. "In fact, it appears that this ion-drive develops power even more slowly than the cesium-fueled type we've been working with ourselves. And if that's the case—"

If that's the case, thought Fairlie, there'll be no trip to the stars for anybody. Maybe this wasn't the stellar drive after all. Maybe it was only an auxiliary unit not worth . . .

The needles on the indicator dials gave a sudden convulsive leap and went off the scales.

In the gorge the sunlight paled. A shaft of blue-violet radiance lanced out from the cliffs at the right side, turning the red-tawny rock to an unnatural purple. It stood like Bifrost Bridge for one eye-blinding moment, its base resting on the opposite cliffs. Then the place where it rested began to erupt in fountains of white fire. Great slabs of rock cracked off and flew wildly about, bounding and clattering. A shock wave hit the bunker, followed by a sonic wave like the end of the world.

Shaken, dazed, and fascinated beyond fright, Fairlie saw the blue-bright shaft slide cantwise down along the wall of rock and then with a terrible skittishness it began to dance, pinwheeling, flicking the walls of the gorge to flame and thunder, leaping skyward, flashing down again at the floor of the gorge which was now filled with dust and the choking clouds of disintegration. Somewhere beyond the greater sounds a tiny thin voice was screaming. And if that force hits the bunker, Fairlie thought, we will have no further worries about stars.

The little voice was crying, "Kill it! Kill it!"

The dancing beam flicked off. Ugly purple turned again to reddish-tawny, lighter where the roiling dust-clouds hung, streaked with a heavier darkness that looked like smoke, as though here and there the rock was burning. A long sliding clattering rumble

51

of thunder continued as parts of the cliffs finished the fall they had irretrievably begun. Then there was a great quiet.

"My God, what happened?" somebody said.

There was a babble of voices.

DeWitt's came clear of the confusion. "It broke loose from the stand," he said. He turned to Thomason. "No perceptible thrust, eh? What do you think about it now?" He grasped Thomason by the front of his shirt and shook him. "What do you think about it now?"

Thomason swore. "I couldn't get any measurement at all. Instruments just couldn't handle it."

"We'll need a new scale of values," Raab said. "A whole new system of calibration. Fairlie!"

Fairlie heard himself say, "Yes?"

"How exactly did you translate the intensity scale?"

"I didn't," Fairlie said, "exactly. The mathematicians postulated it on the basis of what seemed logical to them. I guess they were wrong."

"And small wonder," said Raab. "Controlled energy of that magnitude is quite beyond our present thinking."

"Yes," said Christensen slowly, "and quite beyond our present ability to handle."

DeWitt said, "Not at all. Now that we understand—"

"I don't think we understand anything except that we're playing with something far too big for us. Take a look at that out there." He pointed to the viewports. The dust was settling and the gorge presented an awesome appearance. Great ragged bites were gone out of the cliffs. The rocks were seared, melted, fused, shattered and cast down into smoking rubble. Winstedt measured the distance between the bunker and the nearest edge of the destroyed area and looked sick.

"Just a little bit more," he said, and shivered.

"There will not be any more tests," said Christensen, "until the necessary mathematical work has been done and the test-stands redesigned. Dr. Raab—"

DeWitt said harshly, "Nonsense. We ran this first test too high.

Now we know that we must revise downward. It's as simple as that. Once we get a true reading on our instruments we'll know exactly where we are."

"No," said Christensen. He opened the heavy door of the bunker and went out, into furnace heat and dust-hazed air that smelled of brimstone.

Fairlie followed him. He wanted to get far away from DeWitt and Thomason. Especially DeWitt.

He followed Christensen's massive back along the trail that led to the parking area. He heard voices and footsteps behind him as some of the others began to come out of the bunker. Then suddenly there was a shift in the light and Fairlie froze in his tracks. He saw Christensen spin around in front of him. Behind him a man's voice yelled in sharp alarm. There was a hurried scuffle of feet.

Fairlie turned. Once more a blue-violet Bifrost bridged the gorge, this time from the opposite cliff. It seemed much less brilliant than the first one, but Fairlie did not pause to think about this. He fled back toward the bunker with Christensen's heavy footfalls pounding close behind him.

The blue beam brightened. Fairlie saw the rocks begin to smoke. He put on more speed, remembering the terrible lashing beam of the first generator after it broke loose and thinking what would happen if this one broke loose also and caught him in the open. The bunker was no surety against a direct hit, but it was better than nothing. He flung himself through the door, and Christensen slammed it behind them both.

Fairlie removed himself to the remotest corner he could find and waited for the explosion.

Christensen said, "DeWitt—"

"Quiet!" That was Raab's voice, cold and startling. Christensen stopped with his mouth open. Raab was not looking at him. Fairlie guessed that Raab had not the faintest idea to whom he had spoken and that he could not have cared less. He was bent over his instruments.

"I think I have it now," Raab said. "Increase the intensity

once more, please—careful, that's enough! Now bring it down. Good. Good. Now we have a basis for calculation. Thomason?"

"Good here. Thrust readings are well within range. Thrust potential—I don't believe it, but I know it's true. Holy Aunt Hannah. Right out through the roof."

Beyond the viewport the blue-violet beam hung steady. There was no eruption, no flame, no molten rock. DeWitt spoke, one of the technicians did something, and the beam faded, became almost invisible, then slowly brightened again, brightened, brightened . . .

"That's the danger point," Thomason said matter-of-factly. "Cut it."

The beam flicked out.

Once again there was silence.

Christensen said again, "DeWitt—"

DeWitt said nothing. He smiled in a hard peculiar way and his eyes met Christensen's squarely. The others kept out of it. Raab and Thomason were absorbed in their notes. The technicians were busy removing record tapes and graphs, checking equipment. Winstedt, good politician that he was, slid quietly out the door.

Fairlie thought it was an excellent idea. They walked together along the rocky path.

Winstedt said, "A brilliant piece of work, Dr. Fairlie. I think in the excitement we have all tended to forget who made this possible."

"Thank you," said Fairlie. "It was mostly luck." Luck? It comes in two colors, good and bad. Which one is yours, Fairlie? The drive works and can within crude limits be controlled. The mathematicians, the physicists, the engineers will refine and expand those limits, and it is now certain that the ship will go out.

Is that why Christensen forbade the second test, when he must have known that DeWitt had at least an excellent chance of being right?

Fairlie looked back over his shoulder and saw Christensen walking along the path. In a cold flash of vision, Fairlie found something profoundly moving and symbolic in that solitary figure against the background of the scarred and shattered gorge where the rubble heaps still smoldered, a landscape on the outer shores of Hell.

That image returned to him many times in the days and weeks that followed. Things happened in the outside world, things went forward. DeWitt left the base to superintend the construction of sub-assemblies for a ship. Fairlie understood that the ship would be similar to the lunar rockets but modified to allow for the ion-drive. The construction was top-secret-urgent-in-the-extreme, and when the sub-assemblies were completed they would be brought to the base and combined into the craft that would lift man free of his Earth and into the vast fields of the stars that blazed so brightly every night in the windswept sky.

Fairlie heard about these things, but from far off. Now that his method had been proved the work of translation was progressing with gratifying speed. How it did or why it should was still a mystery, but it was a mystery the linguists had ceased to quarrel with. They let it pass for the time being, completely engrossed in the epic that was beginning to emerge, broken and fragmentary, cryptic, tantalizing, but stunning to the most scholarly emotions, from the records of the Ur-men.

8

A MAN'S STRONG voice spoke out of the depths of space and time. There were authority and pride in it, and a strength that made the resonant phrases echo from the walls of the laboratory, just as before.

But now the words had meaning, and now Fairlie could understand that behind the strength and the pride was something darker—the sure knowledge of defeat.

"It is certain now that our base has been detected, and it is only a matter of time until they will launch the attack. Our small outpost here cannot hope to defend the base against their overwhelming forces and so we have been ordered to abandon it and return to Ryn. Therefore I instruct you to begin evacuation proceedings immediately. But I give you these instructions not in the spirit of cowardice or defeat, but in the certainty that this is only a temporary setback, a small diversion from our path to ultimate victory."

Liar. Valiant liar, Kalber of Ryn. And what happened to you in those final moments when time ran out and "they" caught you with half your forces still in the base and evacuation incomplete? Did you die in the terrible storm that ripped Gassendi, or did you live to limp home with your dead and wounded and your battered ships, to repeat there what you had said already on this recording destined for official ears?

But what about the other recording that was not for official ears, the one in which you spoke from the heart?

"There is no longer any doubt what the final outcome will be. They have beaten us back and back. Soon our last voyage will be done. And after that, until the end of time, they will rule the starways—and any men who venture there will be destroyed. We must cease to look upward. For us now there is nothing but the hard ground under our feet, and no more stars forever."

Three hundred centuries were gone, and still that brief speech, preserved on a sphere of silvery metal, could stab Fairlie's heart with its quiet despair.

No more stars forever.

But who were "they"? What were they like, where did they come from, what were they fighting for?

"We know the Ur-men—or Vanryn, as they called themselves —were humanoid," Lisetti said once, "but what about these 'others'? Nowhere in any of the records is there a word to describe them."

"That's natural enough," said Bogan. "The Ur-men knew perfectly well what they were like—there was no need to describe them. But I imagine that "they" were simply another branch of the same stock, whatever it may have been, fighting for supremacy."

"Perhaps so," said Fairlie. "But then why did Kalber phrase it that way—any *men* who venture there."

"How often do we use the term 'beast' or 'swine' or 'son of a dog'? I doubt whether we're far enough along to believe that we can interpret every subtle shade of colloquial meaning."

And of course Bogan was right.

There was plenty else that they could be sure of. Every scrap of reference to the home-star of the Ur-men was turned over to a team of astronomers, who identified it unquestionably with Altair. After that, on his late night walks from his laboratory to his quarters, Fairlie watched that particular brilliant point of light with a peculiar interest.

On a planet circling that far sun a man named Kalber had been born, and a woman had sung to the stars.

57

If the Moon was up, Fairlie would look at it and shiver. A long way for a man to come to die. If Kalber had died. But certainly others had, and the voice of the woman had lain silent in the cold rock for a long, long time.

Because of "them". And who were "they", the destroyers who would rule the starways and defend them forever against men?

Whoever they were, time had passed for them also. The war was finished thirty thousand years ago, and at this distance what difference was there between the victor and the vanquished? Even ambition has an end.

And yet Kalber had said *until the end of time*.

The sub-assemblies came. DeWitt returned to the base and the ship began building. DeWitt drove Thomason, who needed no driving, and Thomason drove everybody under him. There had been no further trace of the spy or the stolen data, and the various intelligence agencies reported no unusual activities anywhere in unfriendly quarters.

"But whoever got the stuff won't be standing still," DeWitt said grimly. "And he'll be hiding what he does so carefully that only a miracle would give it away."

The ship grew. The records from Gassendi yielded gradually the bases for a whole new technology, not yet fully interpreted nor understood and only partially complete, but enough to light a torch under DeWitt and others like him who dreamed of what might still wait for them under the ruins of whatever civilization had once existed at Altair. Treasures that must be grasped now, quickly and first, before others find them and use them against us, before the starways are closed again by another "them".

Fairlie worked, and tried to ignore the disquieting questions that kept nagging at him.

Then one night Christensen sent for him.

It was a late hour and Fairlie was ready for bed, but the orderly who had come with the jeep and the invitation was quite definite about it. Fairlie pulled on his pants and rode shivering in the chill night to Christensen's quarters, feeling very uneasy all the way. He distrusted any change in routine. It always meant trouble.

58

Christensen met him at the door, an unfamiliar Christensen in a rumpled shirt that hung open over his broad chest, an uncombed unshaven Christensen who smelled like a distillery.

Fairlie stared.

"Yes," said Christensen. "I am veritably and indubitably drunk. Stinking drunk. Will you join me?"

"No thanks," said Fairlie. "I have too much work to do in the morning."

"Mm," said Christensen, and nodded. "The stiff little scholar." He smiled at Fairlie. "Listen to me, stiff little scholar with the disapproving look, and I will tell you something that will crack your academic calm wide open. Sit down, Fairlie. Sit down."

He sat, and Christensen loomed over him. The hair that showed through the open shirt was rough and grizzled like the breast of an old-man gorilla.

"DeWitt spoke to me today," said Christensen. "He wants you for the trip."

"Trip?" said Fairlie stupidly, still occupied with the strangeness of seeing Christensen in this state.

Then Christensen said softly, "Yes, little scholar man. *The* trip." And Fairlie understood.

Christensen sat down and drank, watching Fairlie over his glass.

"That frightens you, doesn't it. Scares the pants off you. Don't lie, I can see it."

"It scares me, yes," said Fairlie. "But why me?"

"You're the youngest and healthiest of our linguists, that's why. And they'll need a linguist, you can see that. Someone like you who can read records, inscriptions. You can even talk the Vanryn language."

Fairlie stared. "Talk the language? The Vanryn language of three hundred centuries ago, yes. But what good would that do? Language changes, in time. It would have changed out of all recognition, by now."

Christensen slopped whisky into a glass and handed it to him. "You look as though you need that drink now. About the lan-

59

guage—yes, it may have changed but it's the old records, the old secrets, DeWitt wants. That's why he wants you to read them." He smiled. "Don't worry, we haven't enough authority to *make* you go. You can still say No."

Christensen paused, staring into his glass. "If I had my way, everybody would say No. There wouldn't be any goddamned lunatic trip to a star—Altair or any other. Not for a long time. Not until—" He stopped.

Fairlie waited, and then he asked, "Until what?"

"That's what DeWitt keeps asking me. What am I waiting for? I don't know. For people to make a little better sense, perhaps. Here we are about to leap for the stars and yet in our minds and emotions we're very slightly changed from the days when he who drew the longest bow ran his brother down, you know— That's roughly Kipling. Didn't know I read poetry, did you? I do. I read a lot of things and the thing that frightens me most is the history of the world. Human history."

Christensen lifted his head and looked at Fairlie. "In your line, you must have read a lot of history. What do you think of it?"

"I've never philosophized about it. As a story of human achievement—"

"And of human folly and human suffering that was mostly about nothing. The martyrdom of Man. And we're still at it, busily hating each other, busily killing because of the writing in some book or the color of a scrap of bunting. Do you know what Winstedt's been working on?"

Fairlie didn't. At the moment he didn't care. DeWitt wants you for the trip, little scholar man. He wants you to go to Altair.

"He's been analyzing some samples—" Christensen broke off and drank again, eyeing Fairlie with a cruel mirth that only partly hid what was behind it. "No, I'll ask you first. Why were your translations successful?"

"We don't know. Sheer coincidence, I suppose. The Vanryn just happened to speak a language that resembled one of our languages."

"Coincidence. But you and I are scholars, Fairlie. We like better explanations than that."

"Do you have one?"

"Winstedt has. Men were killed up there in Gassendi, thousands of years ago. The bodies were removed but there were traces left, smears of blood, bits of tissue, all perfectly preserved. The sun never gets back into that cavern. It's always night, and always cold. Winstedt has been studying them. Chromosomes, blood-types, cell structure, everything."

Fairlie's heart was beating hard and fast. "And?"

"Coincidence is a wonderful thing, Fairlie. Their language vaguely 'resembled' Sumerian. Their bodies more than resembled. They *were* identical with ours, with yours and mine, right here. The chromosomes—you could have married the singing woman, Fairlie, and she'd have given you children, good squalling healthy human brats. How's that for a coincidence, scholar man? And what does it do to all our cherished beliefs? Darwin and Genesis both gone down the drain with one quick pull of the plug." Christensen drank and put the empty glass down. He sat quiet.

Fairlie rose and poured himself a stiff drink from Christensen's bottle. His hands were shaking uncontrollably. "Is he sure about that?"

"Winstedt is an apple-polisher, but he's also a biologist. He's sure."

"Then—" Fairlie sat down again. He felt stunned, and yet somehow not really surprised, as though somewhere in the far back of his mind he had known this all along, felt the kinship between himself and the man Kalber, and the nameless woman who sang of stars. "Then they must have had a colony here," he said. "On Earth."

Christensen nodded. "Gassendi was a guard-post, defending the colony. Makes better sense, doesn't it? And when the base was blasted the colony was cut off. That's only guesswork but the guesses come thick and fast. Maybe we didn't come up from the ape at all, Fairlie. Maybe we came down from the stars instead.

61

That's what scares me the most. I think it's our own past we'll be looking into at Altair."

Our own past. Yes. Back beyond Egypt and the Indus Valley, back beyond Sumer—and will we know now who the Black-headed Ones were and where they came from with their outlandish tongue, to build their mystic mountains upon the plain? And they were none of them new at all but very old, lost children of their star-born fathers, wandering far into the darkness of a savage planet!

And who knows what cities they might have had before Uruk and Mohenjo-Daro, vastly long before, whose walls were trampled to dust by the hairy mammoth or used for hearthstones by Homo Neanderthalensis who was *not* our ancestor. And can we guess now why Cro-Magnon Man appeared so abruptly on the stage of pre-history, full grown and with no connecting link, a whole new species dazzling the hitherto dumb world with the gift of speech—to begin the long climb up again?

Is that why we have always had, from the beginning, this groping hunger for the stars?

We must cease to look upward. For us now there is nothing but the hard ground beneath our feet, and no more stars forever.

But forever is a long time, Kalber. And now we come again.

Fairlie held his head between his hands, feeling the temples throb. Too much to take in, too big. And we don't *know* yet, it may be all a dream, all illusion!

DeWitt wants you, little scholar man. He wants you to go to Altair.

But I can't. I can't go. I'm afraid.

Not even to gain knowledge can I go.

Christensen said, "Do you feel it too?" There were tears in his eyes. "Everything suddenly swept away, knocked out from under." He made a despairing gesture. "Do you feel lost, Fairlie? I do."

9

FAIRLIE WAS looking at a ship. Looking, and not quite believing it.

Not just *a* ship. *The* ship. It rested on its cradle, in the work-area miles from the administrative part of the base. Even thus, supine and with the ant-like figures of men swarming around and over it and in it, there was something about this ship that stirred Fairlie's blood and brought a prickling cold thrill up his spine.

"A new-model lunar rocket," DeWitt said, smiling. "That's what they're working on, as far as they know. What do you think of her?"

"That isn't what you're really asking me," Fairlie said.

"No. I want to know if you've made up your mind."

Fairlie bent his head so that he could not see the ship. "Not yet."

"We expect to begin test flights next week, so you'd better get busy. You understand that if you don't go—"

"I know," said Fairlie irritably. "We can't be allowed to run loose with all our knowledge, so here we'll stay until you get back and all the new discoveries are pawed over and policies are formulated and the general public is gently informed that several things have happened. In other words, I'll be an old man when I'm let out." Dull, he thought. Dull, but safe.

He looked at the ship again. He could not keep his eyes away from it.

"She's more yours than anybody's," DeWitt said. "You gave her to us, in the maintenance-manuals, the plaques and diagrams you translated."

"I remember. I remember something else, too. 'Until the end of time, any men who venture between the stars will be destroyed.'"

"They were men like us. They talked in large terms. Until the end of time—how long is that? Thirty thousand years? Less? More? You sound like an old woman, Fairlie."

"Maybe. And maybe you're overlooking one thing."

"What's that?"

"That when the Vanryn left those manuals and diagrams, *and* the wrecked machines at Gassendi, it meant they didn't worry about those things falling into the hands of their enemies. And why didn't they worry? Only because their enemies had an equal or quite possibly a superior technology."

DeWitt said dryly, "I was able to figure that out." He glanced up, where a lopsided moon rode pale and ghostly in the daylight sky. "The "others", whoever they were, won that battle, and almost certainly they won the whole war. What difference does that make now? There wouldn't be much left of either side."

"Then why go to Altair at all?"

"Because it's there and we can do it," DeWitt said, with as much flippancy as Fairlie had ever seen him muster. He was feeling good these days. "But if that isn't enough for you—and it isn't for me, either—think of what we found in the ruins of an outlying base, and then think what we could learn from the center of that civilization, the home-world."

"Thirty thousand years is a long time," Fairlie said, mockingly.

"All right," DeWitt retorted, suddenly losing his good humor. "Suppose you believe there's nothing left. Suppose *I* believe it. Do we dare to gamble on a supposition that could destroy us if we're wrong? What kind of fools would we be if we said, Oh, it isn't any use, and sat here, and let the other side go out and find that there was plenty left."

Fairlie said, "I'm not going to argue."

"Bogan and Lisetti are too old, Speer's too fat. I've got to have

64

one of you and you're the only one the medics have cleared. Go home and think."

Fairlie did that. Not because DeWitt told him to but because he had to. He closed the windows and shut the blinds. He got cold beer from the tiny refrigerator and turned on the television. He sat with his feet up in the stale, almost-cool gloom and watched the flickering screen.

It was comforting. The raucous inanities of the commercials, the sports announcers who were so honestly excited about the day's baseball scores, the soap-operas about the incredibly vast problems of housewives, the folk-heroes who faced their interminable moment of truth in the dusty western street and always won.

A cheap, busy, blatant, sordid huddle of a world, but for better or worse, mine own. I belong here. I do not belong on a world called Ryn. Even if it was true that the Vanryn were my forefathers instead of the little hairy Earthling we call Proconsul, with his unspecialized hands. It was too long ago. The stuff of this planet is too much a part of my body, my eyes are too well accustomed to its skies.

I have made my decision, he thought. I will stay here.

He felt relieved, clean and comforted.

He watched the televison screen and sipped beer.

I am glad I made that decision, he thought. It was the right one. You can always be sure of a wise decision because no doubts arise to torment you. You are at rest. You *know* you were right.

The television was too loud. He got up and turned down the volume. While he was up he got another beer. When he came back with it the television was still too loud. He turned it down some more. The room had heated up from the sun. He took his shirt off, sat down again, drank more beer, watched the television.

It was becoming very hot. The volume of sound seemed still too high, rasping at his ears and finally at his nerves. He rose and turned the set off.

I need some sleep, he thought. I've lost far too much of it

65

lately, but I can sleep now. My mind is at rest. For the first time I know what I am going to do.

He lay down on the bed and closed his eyes.

He saw the ship. The long beautiful powerful creature that was going out to see the stars.

You go, he said to the ship. You go and welcome.

It was too hot to sleep.

He got up again and walked the narrow space of the floor. A narrow floor, he thought, and the blinds drawn tight and the door locked, and that is my life as it has always been and as it will always be. Because I am afraid to see the ship. Because I am afraid to see the stars.

He lifted the tiny silver sphere from its place, the special sphere that had become tacitly his by right of possession. He placed it carefully on the plastic pin and started the mechanism.

The sphere turned slowly. The woman sang.

Fairlie sat and listened with his head bowed to his hands.

She was not afraid of the stars, he thought. She lifted her arms and called to them, the beautiful fierce burning suns on the other side of blackness. And the blackness was as large and terrible then as it is now, but the woman sang and the men of Ryn went out and were glorious. And their blood and flesh were the same as mine.

Thirty thousand years and the seed has grown again, and the same hunger is in it. The pattern has bred true.

I have made the right decision, Fairlie thought, the wise decision and I know it, but I can't abide by it. Not unless I want to hear this woman's song in my ears as long as I live, a torment and a shame.

So I will take my wise decision and throw it away. I will go. Not gloriously as they went, not proudly with my head high. I will go scared, puking and quavering, knowing myself for a fool, wishing every second for the safe comfort of the closed room I have left behind me. But damn it I will go.

In the ship that is more mine than anyone's because I gave it to them. *I* put the stars in the palms of their hands.

How could I possibly stay behind?

10

FAIRLIE STOOD shivering in the cool night wind and watched the Gassendi rocket come down.

That was not at all what he and the others were here for, but the first flick of orange brilliance caught his eye, high up and brighter than any of the stars. In a few seconds it came again, and now it was lower. Fairlie understood that these were the braking blasts. They came closer and closer together, sliding down the sky, until they melded into a tall pillar of white flame. The thunder rolled down from where the edges of the torn sky slammed together behind the passing hull. A moment later, like a small echo of that thunder, came the hammering of the rockets.

Close beside Fairlie, Christensen grasped the arm of Rendell, the Secretary of Defense, and pointed.

The motion jogged Fairlie out of his hypnotic fascination with pillars of fire. He looked away from the descending rocket, following Christensen's gesture, and in the same quadrant of the sky he saw a shadow moving downward as the rocket moved, but going silently, barely outlined in a flickering of bluish light.

The starship.

He heard someone draw a quick sharp breath. The rocket was crashing down to its landing now, roaring and shaking the earth, but it no longer seemed as mighty and majestic as it had. Beyond it the starship settled as lightly as a blown leaf upon the ground, and the very absence of flamings and thunderings and earth-rockings was proof of a controlled power awesome to contemplate.

The Gassendi rocket cut its jets. In the deafening silence that followed Fairlie saw the faint blue flicker of the starship die, and he stood numbed and speechless, knowing that he had seen one of those moments of history which decisively divides two eras. A new thing had come into the world.

No. Not new. It was sometimes hard to remember that. Hard to remember that ships like this had flown the stars thirty thousand years ago, carrying men who colonized, and fought, and went down to defeat. You knew this, but you had to keep reminding yourself that it was so. Thought-habits ingrained during a lifetime were hard to break.

A jeep went bucketing noisily toward the ship.

"—carefully timed," Christensen was saying, "to coincide with the launching and return of the regular lunar flights, so that foreign radar wouldn't pick up our ship and wonder about it. I hope the trick worked."

Rendell said sourly, "Whoever got hold of those tapes isn't fooled. They'll probably be testing a ship themselves soon, if they haven't already."

Christensen sighed. He turned to Bogan, Lisetti, and Speer, who had watched the landing with Fairlie.

"You had every right to see this, and theoretically you should have every right to know the full results of the test. But you know the situation. Security says that only Fairlie comes beyond this point. So I'll have to ask you to return to your quarters."

Christensen paused, then said heavily, "You've all done a magnificent job."

"And you wish we hadn't," Bogan said. He looked at the shadowy distant bulk of the ship. "I agree with you. A scientist should be concerned only with one thing—adding to mankind's store of knowledge. And yet—there are some additions one would rather not be responsible for."

Speer said, "Just the same, I envy Fairlie."

"That is because you know you are quite safe from going," Lisetti said. He smiled. "Let us go. We are in the way now."

They nodded to Fairlie and got into one of the waiting jeeps and rode away. Fairlie felt very much alone. He tagged awkwardly behind Rendell and Christensen, behind Winstedt and the other top brass, first into a jeep and then into Christensen's office, where he sat in a corner unnoticed while cryptic but very tense and hurried calls were made, chiefly by Rendell. Fairlie thought he was probably talking to the White House but he couldn't be sure. The phone was fitted with a hush device that blanked voices very effectively. After what seemed quite a long time DeWitt came in with Raab and Thomason.

DeWitt shone with a strange hard radiance. There was something almost ferocious about his joy, his triumphant exultance. "The test," he said, "was an unqualified success." He looked around at them, his gaze resting finally on Christensen. The look was a challenge as tangible as the striking of a spear against a shield. "Our reports are ready—you can study them at your convenience, but both Dr. Raab and Thomason will bear me out."

Raab and Thomason made known that they would.

"We've been farther outside the Earth than men have ever been before," DeWitt went on, "since the Ur-men themselves. The drive functions perfectly. All possible preliminary studies have been completed. Dr. Raab and Dr. Thomason agree with me that there will never be a better time than now to initiate our expedition to Altair."

"Then," said Rendell, "I see no reason to delay it further. The final word must come from Washington, of course, but from the conversation I have just had with the White House I think there is no doubt what the word of the Security Council will be. So let us get down to details."

DeWitt said, "As regards the organization of the expedition, I—"

"Yes," said Rendell, cutting him short, "Dr. Christensen will discuss that with you."

DeWitt's face became hard and wary. "Very well. But I would like to remind both you and Dr. Christensen that his authority will end as soon as the ship takes off, and therefore—"

69

Christensen said, "I'm going with you." And he added, "In command."

Fairlie straightened up. He saw DeWitt's look of amazement change to one of cold fury. Thomason, at one side, made a short ejaculation. He looked like a boy who has at the last moment been saddled with a maiden aunt to take to the picnic. Raab looked mildly interested, no more.

DeWitt turned to Rendell. "I protest. This project has been mine from the beginning. I've brought it through in spite of everything Christensen could do to stop me, and now you— It's unfair. It's—" He had no more words.

"I have my authorization," Christensen said quietly, "straight from the White House."

"I see you've been busy behind my back."

Rendell said, "There's more to it than that." There was a sharp little edge to his voice. "Your extreme preoccupation with the necessities of this project has caused you to lose sight of its larger implications."

"Don't bother with the diplomatic English," DeWitt said. "Just tell me what's behind this."

"War," said Rendell. "That's a nice simple word, isn't it? Easily understandable. The charges of an American missile-base in Gassendi have already disturbed the world. If it is learned later on that an American military mission went out to the stars, we'll have the hell and all of a world crisis on our hands."

"But," said DeWitt, showing the edges of his teeth, "I am not a military man."

"You were. And furthermore the whole world knows why you aren't. It would also have a pretty good idea what any expedition led by you was. I have to admit that I question the wisdom of allowing you to go at all, but I realize that there are several reasons why it would be impractical to forbid you. Therefore we have compromised by putting Dr. Christensen in command. I'm sure that whatever your personal feelings may be, you will understand that for the sake of your country, and world peace,

70

it is better that this expedition should be scientific in nature, not military."

DeWitt laughed. It was not a pleasant laugh, nor a humorous one. "What do you think *their* expedition will be for, Rendell? Pure knowledge for the good of mankind, or military knowledge for the good of one nation?"

"I'm rather capable at my job, DeWitt. I know precisely what they'll be after. I also know precisely what they'll *say* they're after."

"No weapons will be snatched out of your hands, DeWitt," said Christensen. "But there are other things to be thought of."

"You're still afraid."

"Yes. I fear the single-minded man, no matter how able."

DeWitt shook his head. "You fear more than that. The future. New ways, new thoughts, things beyond your understanding or control. You're afraid of how we will use them, so you interpose yourself as a block, an obstacle. I'm sick and tired of climbing over you, Christensen." He added cruelly, "You're too old to go. You'll die out there."

Christensen nodded. "Possibly. That doesn't change matters now. Get used to the idea, DeWitt."

They stood looking at each other.

Finally DeWitt said, "All right." He sat down.

Christensen turned to the others. "Gentlemen—"

They all sat down. The discussion began. Fairlie sat with them, joining in when his field became involved but mostly only listening and watching faces.

He was beginning to feel uneasily that the conflict between Christensen and DeWitt might prove to be the biggest hazard that Operation Darkness was likely to face.

71

11

TIME TO PACK. And what do you pack for a trip to the stars?

There are no travel booklets, no helpful advice on climate or social activities, no tips on what luggage is best suited for a starship.

Shaving kit, toothbrush, and aspirin. Those you will need wherever you go. Especially the aspirin. Make it a big bottle.

What else? How many changes of underwear from here to Altair?

Fairlie looked at his open kitbag, the impersonal OD item of lightweight fabric which had been given to him. He put toothbrush, razor, and aspirin into it. He added a comb. Then he sat down in a chair and shook.

As I was going to Altair—

Well, it was your decision. Nobody made you.

Somebody did too make me. That woman. That damned woman who's been dead and dust for thirty thousand years, singing to me, calling to me, and I am a fine one, a real cool hard-headed scientist, to let myself fall for an idiocy like that.

But the song goes with me. Along with the recorder, the vital tapes, the indispensable microfilms of alphabet and vocabulary and all the other stuff that used to seem so vitally important only it isn't now, phonemes and glossematic analyses indeed, and I am a star-rover, the free-handed, the bright-sworded, the hall-forgetter . . .

72

The hell I am. I am a scared fool and if I sit here thinking drivel I will go nowhere but to the psycho ward.

You have to sleep, don't you? Even on a starship? Even on the third world of Altair? All right, then. Get up and get them. Slippers and pajamas.

He got them. He put them carefully in the small bag.

Shorts. Socks. You still have feet and a backside. And T-shirts. Mustn't catch cold with your chest unprotected.

How are laundry arrangements on a spaceship? Do you suds out your scanties and hang them in the bathroom, or do you just go dirty to save water? But I'm forgetting, in a closed system like that no water is wasted by evaporation or any other cause at all. A highly unpleasant thought. I don't care if it is all purified.

I don't want to go. I don't want to go. I don't want to—

Better take the extra pair of reading glasses. You might have trouble getting your prescription refilled out there.

What else?

Handkerchiefs. Of course, handkerchiefs. The Lord only knows what starflight will do to your sinuses.

Now what?

Outer clothing has been provided. There it hangs, a neat functional coverall of some slithery synthetic or other, with built-in heating. I feel like a fool when I put it on, like a two-bit actor in a two-bit unscience fiction movie. I am also afraid of getting a severe shock from my heat-unit, or suppose the thermostat fails.

Don't I get a space-helmet? I'm damned if I'll go without one, it isn't right, it's like an ambulance creeping along twenty miles an hour with no siren. I demand a helmet.

Take a sweater. Mother always said never go anywhere without a sweater.

Poor Mother. Where will her wandering boy be tonight? And I can't tell her. I have to write her a long sweet lying letter about how the Smithsonian is sending me into the Matto Grosso or some damn place and I will be out of touch for a while so don't worry, it is all quite safe and very important work.

73

Well, one part of it is true. I will be out of touch for a while. I will indeed.

No smoking on the ship so I don't have to bother with pipe or tobacco or matches.

Shall I sneak a bottle?

And wind up with it shattered all over your underwear. You've been warned about that. Everything liquid in plastic containers, and the ship's medic will handle the booze supply.

Then I guess I'm all packed. And high time too. Less than two hours before take-off.

And I thought I was doing well to ride that jet out here.

Two hours, and what will I do with them? Go talk to Speer and Lisetti and the great Bogan who is not so great any more because the foundations of his world have been smashed to pieces and partly by his own hand? Good men, good scholars, good citizens. But I do not wish to spend the time with them.

I wish to be alone with Earth.

I never understood before how much she and I have in common. It is reminiscent of the familiar fictional situation of the man who does not know he is in love until he leaves the woman in question. I wish to be with Earth, to look at her face, to feel her warmth, to smell her perfume, the dry bitter-sweet dust-and-sage that she wears here. I want to watch the sun go down beyond the rim of her mountains.

Two hours in which to remember all the things about Earth that I have forgotten since I was a child full of the wonder of green grass and running streams. The stone walls closed in on me and I forgot.

No, I closed them in upon myself. But I forgot. And now it is time to remember.

Fairlie went out of the bungalow. He walked alone to a rise of land and sat by himself on the crest of it until the sun went down. Then he came back and dressed himself in the coverall and waited until the jeep came to get him and his kitbag and his box of tapes and microfilms. He rode in the jeep to the place where the ship waited, the high slim soaring shadow in the night.

74

There was a strange peacefulness on him now. It was as though a part of his mind had been uncoupled, so that there was no longer any interlocking of thought and emotion.

Fairlie did not feel anything. He was able to perform simple functions like getting into the jeep and getting out of it again, like going through the routine of identification and then walking the rest of the way to the loading area. He was able to think, looking up at the ship in the arms of its gantry, *It seems to be standing on tiptoe.* He was able to speak to the men he met though he was not sure who they were, and anyway it was a matter of no importance.

When he was told to get into the bucket lift he got into it, and rode upward looking out mildly over the desert land. Once he looked at his hands grasping the bucket rail and wondered why they were shaking so; it occurred to him that he was cold and he thought that he would put on his sweater once he got inside.

There was an opening in the wall where the bucket stopped. He went through it into a circular corridor walled with dully-gleaming metal. Somebody called him by name and took him into a room where some other men were already lying on strange-looking beds. The somebody told him to lie down here and he did on one of the beds, it was very comfortable but he did not quite like the way it wrapped itself around him like a sort of spongy quicksand. It had the feeling of a trap. A faint far pang of alarm quivered suddenly at the back of his brain.

Fairlie started to get up, but padded clamps already held him by the chest, the hips, the ankles. He yelled. At the same instant he felt the prick of a needle in his arm. Somebody told him soothingly to relax, everything was all right. The somebody lied, everything was not all right and he knew it. But a pleasant lassitude swept over him, loosening his rigid muscles, smoothing away the fear. He floated in a hazy warmth and it was all very nice now.

He slept. And in his sleep he had a dream. He dreamed that he lay warm and drowsy on a mountain peak in the sun. Sounds rang hollow and far away around him; he did not know what they were but they did not concern him and he paid no attention to them. Then the sunlight began to go. It vanished out of the sky and the sky was dark and he began to fall up into the darkness, up and up faster and faster pushing through the air and the air piled on top of him and it was heavy, it pressed and crushed upon him and the speed of his upward falling was so great that the breath was sucked from his lungs. A great dull sound filled the universe, too deep and low for true hearing, he heard it with his bones rather than his ears. His nose gushed a sudden fountain of wetness and he knew it was blood. He died with the taste of it in his mouth.

There was, unfortunately, a resurrection.

It came slowly, creeping through sore and outraged flesh, along the painful skeleton with every articulation stretched to the snapping point. Part of it clotted in the stomach and stayed there, a squirming lump of sickness. The rest of it reached the skull and packed itself in until the temples bulged and the brain-pan cracked.

Fairlie opened his eyes.

It was a mistake, but once made there was no calling it back. The room appeared to him like the emergency ward of a hospital right after a train wreck, full of writhing figures who groaned. Somebody moved quickly among the weird-shaped beds. Fairlie caught the flash of a syringe. He thought the groaning tapered off as the man moved but he was too occupied with his own misery to care much. Then a man's face appeared above him and smiled cheerily. The smile was oddly gruesome because the man's face was white as chalk except where dark red smears remained beside the nose and at the corners of the mouth.

"Getting a little reaction, aren't we?" said the face inanely. "This will take care of it." Flash, jab, another squirt of something into the protesting vein. "Just lie still for a few minutes."

The face disappeared. Fairlie lay still. Gradually the sickness, the soreness, the skull-splitting ache all receded, not quite to the vanishing point but close enough. He could think again.

And that was bad, because now he realized where he was.

Above the mountain peaks. Above the sky. Above the Moon,

high in the blackness of nothing, with void below and void overhead and all around.

Fairlie grew sick again. He wanted to vomit and he couldn't, the damned drugs wouldn't let him. He wanted to cry but he couldn't do that either. He lay with his eyes shut and suffered.

Earth was gone, dropped behind him like a child's ball into the vastness of a Grand Canyon with no bottom.

He had a vision of it, spinning vertiginously away and downward, and it was more than he could stand. He shook his head violently and sat up, looking at the metal walls that closed him in, the smooth solid floors beneath his feet. He held his thoughts resolutely within that enclosed space, being thankful that there were no windows.

Others were sitting up now, making the same painful effort to grasp the reality of what had happened to them. We're all in the same boat, Fairlie thought, and isn't it wonderful how the human mind can think in cliches even on its way to the stars?

But it was true in more senses than one. Every face showed the same hollow, frightened look, the same appalled understanding. Even Thomason, tough Thomason the steely engineer, looked like a lost kid about to howl for his mother.

Beside him Raab sat on the edge of his recoil couch and rubbed fastidiously at his face to remove the evidences of nose-bleed. He did not appear to be disturbed by anything but the physical discomforts of the situation, which would naturally affect the functioning of the brain. And yet Fairlie caught one glance from him that proved this was not so—even Raab could not completely ignore his Earth-born humanity.

Fairlie wondered how it was with DeWitt and the men who actually worked the ship. They were all handpicked from the Gassendi crews. They had all been in space before, and even though this was different the experience might help to soften the shock. But for the civilian scientists aboard, sedentary men like Fairlie, the shock of separation was shattering.

And it was like starting down a toboggan slide. Once you got going you couldn't change your mind and turn back.

The doctor was moving busily, checking pulse rates and blood pressures, making notes. His name was Reicher. He was young and his face had already regained most of its color. Winstedt still clung to his couch, looking like a collapsed paper bag. Reicher checked him twice, assured him he was all right, and passed on. There was an astrophysicist beyond him, a reasonably young man named Wiley, and beyond him a geologist and a mathematician whose names Fairlie could not remember.

Beyond them Christensen sat on his couch with his head in his hands. There was something about the sagging, quiescent posture of the great broad body that woke a sudden pity in Fairlie. Reicher spoke to him but he did not answer. He spoke again, and this time Christensen looked up with a slow dazed look and said, "I'll be all right. Just let me alone."

Reicher said, "Lie down. I want to check you."

"No." Christensen put his hands down on the couch and braced himself, and managed to get onto his feet. He pushed Reicher away when Reicher tried to help him. His eyes were still dazed and Fairlie thought he was operating chiefly on instinct and courage, but he looked around at them all and smiled, a curious and crooked smile.

"Isn't anyone," he asked, "going to make the appropriate, unforgettable remark about man's returning to the stars?"

After thirty thousand years, thought Fairlie. Back to the forgotten home long lost in the debacle of a forgotten war.

Is the hearth still swept and the fire burning, awaiting our return? Did they survive, our brothers of Altair? Or was everything shattered and destroyed as it was at Gassendi? If they do live, will they remember us, will they remember Kalber and the others by a little yellow star a long way off?

Thirty thousand years.

Who knows?

In spite of his sickness, in spite of his fear, Fairlie's heart began to beat with a powerful excitement.

78

12

THE EXCITEMENT did not last long.

Fairlie sat with Christensen, Winstedt, and DeWitt in the small functional lounge room that served them for every activity but sleeping. They took turns at it, arranging sleeping hours so that only half the personnel was on deck at any one time and then reshuffling the groups so that there was a change of faces. After a sufficient number of shufflings all the faces became repugnant and all the conversation unbearably familiar.

"Is it possible," Fairlie asked, "to be bored on a flight to Altair?"

"The human animal is infinitely adaptable," Winstedt said. "It's not only possible. It's inevitable."

DeWitt said, "I'm not bored. Just waiting." He smiled and stretched his arms, then settled again into his chair. He's telling the truth, Fairlie thought. He's like a cat, rested, relaxed, patient, letting the time go by.

"That's because you know what you're going for," said Christensen, "and you're convinced you're going to find it. That's the one advantage of the single mind. No doubts, no uncertainties. No second thoughts. The rest of us—" He glanced around. "We don't know."

Winstedt grunted. "Philosophical considerations aside, I am sick of looking at the same damned walls, eating the same damned

79

tasteless food, doing nothing but eat, sleep, and sit. How much longer, DeWitt?"

DeWitt grinned and shook his head. "Who knows? Since we passed the light-barrier we're technically nowhere, and there's no time in nowhere."

"The chronometers still work."

"Sure. They're mechanical, they measure the same intervals they always did. But how do we know what the intervals mean here? How do we know how much our own time-sense has been distorted? We're outrunning light and that means that in a sense we're outside of ordinary time."

Winstedt nodded. "And I'm sure the math boys are having fun with the problem. Meanwhile I'd just like to know how much longer I will be cooped up in this trap."

"Well," said DeWitt, "the Ur-men used an arbitrary system as a point of reference in computing time on these voyages. By their reckoning, about three more weeks until we re-translate into normal space and see how close we came to hitting Altair."

Christensen said, "What happens if your calculations are wrong, if the translation of the mathematical symbols was just a fraction in error?"

Fairlie had heard that question before. Christensen seemed to be fond of asking it.

DeWitt said softly, "Go ahead, Chris, needle all you want. Hope all you want. We'll make it."

"I'll make it, too."

"Did I say you wouldn't?"

"Once. And every time you meet me you look into my face with that intent and hopeful look." Christensen smiled. "I'm not going to make it that easy for you."

Don't be too sure, thought Fairlie, and resolutely looked away from Christensen. The strain had been hard on all of them. The violent wrench of take-off, the unavoidable mental anguish that built with the building of the drive-potential, wondering what would happen when they crossed that uncrossable barrier of light-speed, feeling horribly alone and lost. Then the plunge into the nameless hyperdimension, guided by nothing at all but a set of equations, symbols, and directives worked out thirty thousand years ago and strained into modern English through the doubtful brain tissues of one Fairlie. After that the unnatural aspects of the life aboard this ship that was not a ship at all but a tightly-sealed trap, became even more hideously unnatural.

Briefly they had seen the stars. They had looked out upon the universe and seen it as God saw it, an incredible vastness swarming with suns and galaxies of suns, beautiful with a billion billion lights shining purely in the clean dark, and it was terrifying but it was not dull. Not in the least dull. But the tremendous power of the drive hurled them faster and faster, building velocity until the stars were distorted and drawn out into strange lines and finally into a nightmarish and unreal gloom that gnawed at the mind.

The ports were closed. They sat blind inside the ship and felt curious and unpleasant changes taking place in themselves, in their time-sense, in the action of their blood, the beating of their hearts. There were some odd reactions. Dr. Reicher wallowed in a perpetual feast of aberrations, hallucinations, pseudo-ataxias and psycho-pathologies of the most exotic sort. Everybody used opiates to sleep, and still they had nightmares.

It was hard. Mentally and physically hard on everybody, even on DeWitt, though he showed it less than anyone. But it had been hardest of all on Christensen. He had lost weight. His face was grayish, his eyes deep-sunk and shadowed. Fairlie suspected that he had sustained some serious physical damage in the take-off, the strain perhaps aggravating some latent condition that might never have bothered him if he had stayed on Earth. Reicher was worried about him, Fairlie knew, though nothing had been said out loud.

Perhaps, thought Fairlie, when we land he'll pick up again. And he was surprised to find how much Christensen had come to mean to him. During the voyage, as he had watched DeWitt and listened to him, he understood more and more how vitally important it was to have a man like Christensen in command. If anything happened to him it could be very bad both for the

81

expedition and for the world, maybe even for two worlds. In a situation where anything at all might happen, where they could not even guess at what they might find on a totally strange planet, it needed a man with judgment and the ability to see more than one side to a problem.

There was more to it than that, though. Fairlie liked Christensen as a man. He had had more opportunity to know him here, where the close confinement threw people together whether they would or not. He had talked with him, glimpsed something of the complexities underlying the hearty Viking exterior. Christensen was a thinker and Fairlie believed that that as much as the physical strain was tearing Christensen to pieces.

DeWitt had his problems, his strains and stresses, but they were all on one level. He could deal with them. Christensen was different. Vast areas of thought and conjecture were open to him that DeWitt never heard of, and the farther he wandered in them the harder it got. Fairlie had done some wandering himself. He felt for Christensen. He hoped very much that nothing would happen to him.

The watch came to an end. Fairlie was always glad when they ended and he could go to sleep because time passed so much more quickly in sleep. This feeling of gladness lasted until he actually lay down on the couch waiting for the opiate to take effect. Then he began to think about the nightmares and wish he could stay awake until the voyage was over. He always tried hard not to think of the nightmares just before he went to sleep because he was sure that helped to bring them on, but it was difficult not to think of them. There was even a perverse fascination about them, they were so strange and vivid.

They began usually in the drowsy interval just before sleep, when the censor band relaxed and things crept across it that were usually suppressed. He would think of the ghostly nothingness in which they moved—and *did* they move really? There was no sense of motion at all. There was no sense of anything except the whine and throb of the generators and the mechanical noises of the ship. Did they simply hang frozen in some weird stasis while

82

the universe revolved around them like a huge roulette wheel, waiting to drop the ship into the slot marked ALTAIR?

He would see this from the outside, the ship and the flickering insane whirl of stars and space-time around it, and he would feel cold and sick with dizzy terror. Then he would think of Kalber. He would think of all the men of his race who had conquered this nothingness long ago. He would think of the woman and her song, and the pride, the exaltation would sweep over him in a warm bright wave and he would feel like a conqueror, like a god.

Then he would remember the war.

He would think of war in this nothingness.

He would think of death in this nowhere out of space and time.

He would think of those nameless Others hunting and hounding through the eerie void, seeking out the ships, destroying them, making not the brightness and the song.

He would hear the voice of Kalber. *They will rule the starways, and any men who venture there will be destroyed.*

No more stars forever.

And here we are, he would think. Thirty thousand years, and here we are, and where are they—and do they still rule the starways? Are they there outside, somewhere in nowhere, watching us in the gloom while the galaxy spins flickering around?

He would carry these thoughts with him into sleep, and in his dreams he would see the great abyss in which they travelled as a place haunted by all those very many men who had died here in battle long ago, the men who never saw the sun again. And they were not alone, those shades. The enemy was still there, a darksome presence hovering always just beyond the edge of sight. In his dreams he would know that they were there, he could feel the coldness of them, the immense power, but he could never see them.

He was sure, in his dreams, that they saw him.

He would try to run from them in the nothingness, but there was nothing to tell him whether he moved or not. Motion was a mockery, like time. He would try to hide from them but there was no place to hide. He would feel them gathering about him, he would hear them whispering. He would draw himself then into a tight-curled huddle with his arms around his head, but it was no use, their eyes peered and their voices whispered and then the last horrible knowledge would come to him that they were not outside at all, not outside of him but inside of him, moving stealthily along the corridors of his brain, rustling, poking, prying, questioning.

That was when somebody would shake him brutally awake and tell him to shut up.

The dream did not, fortunately, reach this ultimate point too often.

The strange part of it was that at some time or another it reached that point for every one of them.

Reicher was not impressed. "We all have the same knowledge of the Ur-men and the war they fought," he said. "We've all done the same sort of speculation on the nature of the enemy. We are all here scared to death of the same thing—the Unknown—and we're all subject to the same physical and mental effects of this unnatural environment. I don't see how we could possibly avoid sharing the same hallucinations to a very considerable degree."

Logical, Fairlie thought. Quite logical. And probably quite true. But—

He discussed the dreams with Christensen once.

"I hope the doctor is right," Christensen said. "Because what I feel when they come near me, when they examine my mind, turning my thoughts over one by one—" He paused. "What I feel is power, and not human power, and I would rather think that it is an illusory sensation caused by some sort of physical stimulus."

"Yes," said Fairlie. "So would I."

"I imagine we'll know for sure pretty soon."

Fairlie looked at him. "How?"

"When we leave this—this ultra-dimension, get back into normal space and time, land on a solid physical world. If the hallucinations stop—well, then, that's all they were. But if the effect goes with us after the stimuli are gone—"

Fairlie shivered. "Damn it," he said. "I wish you hadn't brought that up."

He had been looking forward with such longing to the day Christensen spoke of. He had almost ceased to care what they found on the third world of Altair just so long as they found it and there was air to breathe and solid ground underfoot.

Now he was not so sure.

13

ALTAIR BLAZED in the void ahead of them, a great yellowish-white diamond turning, turning, shooting fire from every facet as it turned. Fairlie looked at it through the shielded port. He had no words. He did not even have any thoughts. He was drowned in splendor.

The ship moved in toward the sun.

A planet came spinning through the field of light. At first it was only a tiny fleck of brightness but it leaped and grew at fantastic speed, first to a ball and then to a sphere that continued to grow and change, taking on new colors, showing at last the dim outlines of continents and seas, a haze of sky, the upper surfaces of cloud-masses blinding bright.

Ryn, the third world of Altair.

Ryn, the world of my forefathers, Fairlie thought, and what will it be like, this homecoming after thirty thousand years?

The planet became a disc, filling the whole port.

Fairlie looked over at Christensen and smiled. "We made it."

The bones of Christensen's face stood out, with the pale skin stretched over them. He looked a hundred years old, sitting there watching this alien world swing toward them in its orbit around an alien sun. Alien, and yet not alien.

Christensen said, "Yes, we made it."

"And I haven't had any more nightmares. Have you?"

"Not those particular ones. No."

The effect had not followed them out of hyperspace. Fairlie had slept in peace, unhaunted and unpursued. Everybody else had, too, and he was sure now that Reicher's diagnosis of shared hallucination had been correct. Morale had shot up astonishingly with the return to normal space. People stopped having symptoms and became euphoric as spring lambs with the prospect of landing.

The ship stirred and muttered, taking the feel of gravity, fighting against it. Fairlie glanced again at Christensen, this time anxiously.

"I know landing isn't supposed to be as rugged as taking off but it feels as though it could get rough even so. Hadn't you better lie down?"

Christensen's gaze was fixed on Ryn, on the face of a new world. "No," he said.

"At least let the doctor give you a shot."

"I've come a long way to see this, Fairlie. I won't be coming this way again. I don't want a shot."

The disc widened and ceased to be. Now there was a surface, wrinkled, humped, shaded in green, in gray and brown and sand-color.

The ship's generators pounded, whining, braking the inward plunge. Fairlie clung to his chair, feeling himself now pressed into the padded back, now flung against the safety harness. It made him dizzy and it was a labor to breathe, but it was quite bearable.

He watched the up-falling of a world.

There was an ocean, flashing like a heliograph in the sun. It tilted and slid away under them and the sunlight faded around the curve of the planet and it was night. There were two moons. The tops of the clouds reflected their light brilliantly. The dark land rolled beneath them. Forest, Fairlie thought, and open plain from the look of it, sloping up again to a mountain chain with snow all a-glitter on the highest peaks. Strangely familiar. Strangely like Earth.

They came out of shadow into light again, spiralling in, dropping down.

Close enough to see, after a while, if there were cities or patterns of roads or broad areas of cultivation.

There were not.

Mountains, hills, plains, and rivers. Rolling prairies and desert, almost every kind of terrain showing as the ship angled across the bulge of the equator, over the white flat waste of the southern pole, north again across land where Fairlie expected water, and water where Fairlie expected land. And it was all empty, fresh and clean as though man had never seen it.

Fairlie glanced at Christensen and saw his eyes brilliant with a secret emotion. He thought that it was hope.

Once more it was night.

Once more the two moons poured an eerie glimmer across the darkness. Empty darkness. Fairlie stared down into it, feeling with Christensen that it was better this way, to find a world with no one and nothing in it—one could forget the fears and the problems. One could forget DeWitt and weapons and possible wars and think only that a great voyage had been made. But at the same time he felt disappointed and depressed. Irrationally, he wanted there to be people.

Bands playing? Flags flying? Cries of *Welcome home, brothers from across the galaxy?*

The eternal child, he thought. Look at me, look what I did, appreciate me. Well, all right. But rocks and trees are so damned uncaring.

He wondered what DeWitt was thinking, up there in the control room staring at an empty world and seeing his visions crumble into the dust of thirty thousand years.

Better so, much better. We have weapons enough, both sides of us. Weapons a-plenty. And if there are none for us there will be none for them either when they get here.

The dark land fled past beneath them, giving back only an occasional gleam of moonlight from some quiet lake.

Then Christensen gave a low cry and in the same instant Fairlie thought he saw a flicker of light in the night below.

Not light.

Lights.

They vanished behind the swift rush of the ship, leaving only an impression of reddish-yellow pinpoints grouped together.

Christensen said, "Did you see it?"

"I saw it."

"A town?"

"I don't know." It seemed important to reassure Christensen. "Probably not. Could be a lot of other things, fire, volcanic action, maybe just a trick of refraction."

Christensen was not reassured. "Whatever it was, DeWitt won't rest until he finds out." He shut his eyes. "For a while there I thought— But I guess we aren't going to find it that simple."

After a while he added, "I guess we couldn't expect it to be."

The ship plunged over the rim of morning. And as though it had been waiting for them to find it, they saw the huge fused blackened scar in the midst of the tawny plain, and between the scar and the low hills beyond they saw the wild grasses interspersed with scattered stone in a way that was unmistakably not natural.

And here they landed.

There was a period of waiting while various tests were run. It seemed obvious that the colonizing Vanryn would have chosen planets as similar as possible to their own native world, and that therefore by reverse reasoning their descendants on Earth would be perfectly able to live in comfort on Ryn. But no chances were being taken.

During the wait DeWitt came to the lounge for a meeting with Christensen. Winstedt, Raab, and Thomason were there, and Fairlie. Outside the port it was mid-morning. The yellowish-white sun shone, wind rippled the grass in long running waves to the edge of the black scar where all life stopped.

It might, Fairlie thought, have been Kansas on a fall morning, except that everything was subtly wrong. The whiter sun made the sky a coppery color by contrast or refraction. The tints of soil and grass were not right, nor the shapes of things—a shrub, a tree, the grass-blades themselves, a sudden flight of strange birds as big as geese winging low with plumage like blue fire.

89

It was not Kansas. It was not Earth.

"I think we ought to agree on a plan of action," DeWitt said. "And I think we might as well be honest, too. You're not well, Chris. You're not physically able to lead any expeditions. So I would suggest we vote on a change of—"

"I'm still on my feet," said Christensen. "I plan to stay that way. There will be no change of leaders."

DeWitt said softly, "So you saw the lights too."

"There's no proof that they were man-made."

"But you think they might be. If the planet was totally ruined and empty you wouldn't care, you'd be glad to take to your bed and rest. But you're afraid."

Christensen turned toward the port. "Look out there. Tell me what made that hideousness."

DeWitt continued to look levelly at him for a moment, and then turned and glanced almost indifferently at the black farspread blotch that glistened faintly with a glassy shine in the sunlight.

"We won't know what did that until we make some tests," he said. "But we can make a pretty good guess. Probably the same type of weapon that destroyed Gassendi."

"And after all this time not a single blade of grass will grow." Christensen shook his head. "What was here before that weapon struck? A great city, I would guess, covering half this plain, and a starport covering the other half, where the ships came and went. One blow, and now there is nothing. Doesn't that frighten you when you think of it, DeWitt?"

"Yes, it does. It frightens me to think of such power in anybody else's hands. That's why I want to find it first." DeWitt's voice was brutal with impatience. "You're a dreamer, Chris. You think if you don't want war it won't come. You think it will respect your wishes. I tell you it isn't a matter of wanting war or not wanting it. I tell you it's a matter of self-defense. If a man comes at me with a big club, I want by God a bigger one to hit him back with."

Christensen said heavily, "There's sense in that. I admit it.

90

But there are other considerations." He paused, then said slowly, "We'll explore this immediate locality first. If there are people they may contact us here. If not, we'll try and find those lights again. Oh, and DeWitt—"

Very softly. Soft as the paw of the tiger before the strike.

"What?"

"If there are people, remember that this world belongs to them. We didn't bring a ship back to the stars just to start up another war, even a small one." He turned around to face DeWitt, smiling a hard smile. "And remember, they might be the ones with the biggest club."

14

THE TESTS WERE satisfactory, to no one's surprise. Atmosphere, pressure, gravitation, temperature, and radiation count were all slightly different from Earth's constants but all of them were well within the limits of tolerance. They could open up the hatches and step out.

They did. And for the first time the true alienage of the planet hit them full force and head on.

Chiefly, Fairlie thought, it was the sunlight and the colors. Altair burned white-tinged-with-yellow in a coppery sky, and all the landscape ran to tawny reds and shades of gold and brown and very odd greens. The coloring of the clouds was superbly impossible.

After that it was shapes and textures. You picked a handful of grass or a spray of leaves or a crimson flower and you knew that they were grasses and leaves and a flower. But they were unfamiliar. They did not even smell right and that too was a strangeness, the wind blowing across the world and bringing with it the very breath of the unknown.

There were sounds, small rustlings and cryings and callings. Unseen things stirred in the grasses and among the stones and there was no way of knowing what they were, whether harmless or deadly, until they were caught and studied.

It's beautiful, Fairlie thought. *It's beautiful, and strange, and for God's sake what am I doing here?*

It remained to be seen what the bacteria would do to them, Winstedt said. In the meantime they would take antibiotics and hope.

By the second day after landing, preliminary preparations were going forward nicely. The towering ship, their base and home, was the center of antlike activity.

The light helicopters and trac-cars, stowed in disassembled form, had been unloaded and were being assembled. Reicher had thoroughly tested the water and pronounced it good. Winstedt, commandeering all the help he could get, had plunged into work in this biologist's paradise and hell.

Not until then did Christensen, with DeWitt and Fairlie and the other two specialists who had no urgent work at this moment, Raab and Thomason, start out for a look at the broken stones beyond the black scar. With them went Graeme, the chief flight officer, and a husky young flight technician named Smith.

They walked. The black fused material of the scarred area had millions of infinitesimal cutting surfaces that abraded skin or leather like tiny razors. They avoided it. It was a bleak ugly thing, reminder of ancient violence, ancient agony. This was part of the battleground, Fairlie thought. Men died here, and their dying left a mark a hundred miles long. What a day it must have been, the day it happened.

"We'll know a lot more when the films have been processed and studied," DeWitt said. The mapping cameras had been operating, of course, during every moment of their landing spiral. "With any luck they should show us the position of those lights. In the meantime we're trying all radio frequencies, in the hope of making some contact."

Thomason grunted. "Fat chance. Doesn't look to me as though there was a human soul left alive on the whole damn planet."

Looking all around with his slow cold gaze, Raab said absently, "Total destruction here. Total. A very important objective, I would judge."

"From the air you could get some idea of the extent of the city," DeWitt said. He swept his hand in a wide arc. "It must have been tremendous, bigger than anything we have on Earth. And this black area— The old war seems to have been fought over star-travel and I think that this must have been the center of the thing for the Vanryn, their main starport. The enemy saw to it that they didn't fly again."

DeWitt looked at the time-eaten stones that once had been a city, hungrily, fiercely. "There may be something left. Somewhere. Underground, perhaps. Surely they would have had vaults or shelters."

Fairlie could see nothing himself but lumps of scattered stone lost in wild grasses and creepers.

He felt a strange sadness when he thought that perhaps here, on this very spot, the woman who sang had lived. How many people here had listened to her singing, with the great starport behind them and the bright stars that were their realm looking down upon them? But that was before the Vanryn pride and the Vanryn glory had been broken.

Christensen was looking back at the ship, reared up like a tower in the plain between the black scar and the first ragged flanks of ruin.

"It looks terribly exposed, doesn't it?" he said. "Out there in the open."

DeWitt grinned briefly. "Still trying to frighten me with thirty-thousand-year-old bogey-men. Well, there's been no sign of them and I don't think there will be. Time wins every war, Chris. But I'll tell you something. I'd be glad to know they did still exist, and I'd be glad to meet them. The Vanryn had a technology that in some ways makes ours look childish, and yet the enemy beat them, crushed them, swept them clean out of space. Think what *their* technology must have been! Think of the things they could teach us."

"Yes," said Christensen. He looked back once more at the ship, and was silent.

This was only the first preliminary survey. They could not hope to cover any appreciable area of the vast ruin on foot, but

94

they could at least get some idea of what they might expect to find.

"Look for inscriptions, Fairlie," DeWitt said. "Anything, even one word, even part of a word."

They walked slowly among the ruins in the yellow sunlight, under the copper sky. The tawny grasses whispered around their ankles, shaking out a sweet dry smell. Small and distant from the ship came the sounds of human activity, clangings and poundings, the thin screek of winches, a shouted voice. They seemed only to point up the silence.

Far and far away on all sides the rough lumped bones of the city were scattered under the uncaring sky, and Fairlie was reminded of a feeling he had had when he visited certain archaeological digs on Earth—how young, how recent, Mohenjo-Daro and Hatti, Nineveh and Thebes, cities only a pinpoint away in time compared to this one! A feeling that a place where there had once been a busy active center of life which was now gone had a quality of loneliness never found in virgin wilderness. That loneliness was here, more vast and moving than any he had known before.

Even young Smith felt it. "You know what I feel like?" he asked of anybody that might be interested. "I feel like I'm walking through a graveyard."

"And you are," Christensen said. "Just that."

The Gassendi base, which had presumably been destroyed much earlier than this place on the home-world, had remained intact even to pieces of cloth and paper, but that was on the sterile Moon where nothing ever changes. Here there were wind and rain, oxidation, bacteria, the ceaseless working of decay. The time-gnawed stones retained no semblance of their former shape or usefulness. Rusty red smears among the grass-roots appeared once to have been metal. That was all. Storm and flood, wind-drifted dust and natural erosion had filled the pits and hollows and brought the high places crumbling down until it was all one level nothingness.

95

"You won't find any inscriptions here," Fairlie said. "Probably not anywhere, but certainly not on the surface."

DeWitt stood with his shoulders hunched and his jaw set, looking around at the ruins with the same look he had given the alien records and the tapes all those eternities ago on Earth. Rip it out, tear it out, make it give up its secret.

"We'll dig," he said. "Aerial photography may give us an idea where the center of the city was, the government buildings where the important records were kept. Maybe the vaults would have held all right, especially if they were sunk in rock. We'll dig."

"You'd better be lucky," Fairlie said. "A job like that could take you more years than any of us have left."

DeWitt glowered at him and turned back.

Christensen had been sitting on a stone. He looked exhausted and his breathing was labored.

"You shouldn't have come," said Fairlie.

Christensen smiled and shook his head. "As long as I'm leader I have to come." He gave his hand to Fairlie to be helped up, and Fairlie was shocked at the bony weakness of it.

"Does it strike you as odd," Christensen said, "that the city itself was apparently not touched by enemy action? I've been sitting here and thinking. What we assume to have been the starport was simply erased forever out of existence, but it's as though the city simply crumbled away because there was no longer any use for it. Do you suppose the enemy had some humanitarian impulses?"

"It's possible. Of course we don't know how much of the population had already perished. But still, from the way Kalber spoke, he didn't seem to expect total annihilation, just the end of all star-voyaging." He paused, then added, "Which might have been about the same thing for the Vanryn."

They walked back toward the ship, slowly because of Christensen. Fairlie watched DeWitt striding ahead with Thomason, the two broad blocky heads close together, the two sets of square implacable shoulders moving as they planned to rip the winding-sheet from the bones of the city.

"It's no use to tell them," Fairlie said, "but I think they're likely to have their work for their pains. The chances are very small that the survivors of the destruction would have stayed here. I think they would have moved their capital to another place. Total defeat and a complete reshaping of their culture would have been hard enough to cope with, without clinging to a corpse —if you know what I mean."

Christensen said, "Let him waste all the time he wants to. There's a limit on how long we can stay, a limit on fuel supplies for the machines. The less time he has the less trouble he can make."

Fairlie looked all around at the empty plain, the rim of hills with patches of forest on their flanks, the winding of a placid river, the empty sky.

"Do you still think there are people here?"

"Let's say I'm not at all sure there aren't."

"They certainly haven't been in any rush to get in touch with us."

"Maybe," said Christensen, "they don't want to."

15

DeWitt had been digging for three days and two nights and this was the beginning of the third night. Fairlie sat on a stone and watched sourly. He was tired and the wind was cold, and he was sick of DeWitt and his driving purpose. He was sick of Thomason too. He was rapidly getting sick of Ryn. The whole business was bogging down in stupid anticlimax.

Working with the light scoops attached to the half-tracs, DeWitt and Thomason and their crew had made a sizable hole in the ground. They had picked their spot from the air, where the configuration of the ground seemed to indicate the foundation lines of a complex of unusually large buildings. Now parts of the foundations had been laid bare. They were in very bad shape, but the miracle was that they had survived at all, in any form. Thomason said the material was some sort of plastic-like cement with the water-resistant properties of glass, so that deterioration had been incredibly slow. The Vanryn had built for the ages. But this age had been too long, even for them.

Floodlights blazed, casting harsh shadows among the ruins. Heaps of dirt lay about, filled with unidentifiable rubble, bits of stone. The scoops gnawed carefully away at more of the same in the excavation. So far there was no sign of a vault. So far there was no sign of anything.

DeWitt was by no means ready to give up.

"We'll just move and dig someplace else. Sooner or later we'll turn up something. There's got to be something left."

"Why?" asked Fairlie. "Because you say so?" He got up. "Call me if you find a large inscription. I'm going back to the ship."

He walked away. For a while he had a long shadow going before him. Then as the blot of hard light became more and more remote the shadow dwindled and faded into the last dark dusk that was on the land. The starship stood up with a lean stark beauty against the copper-glowing sky. In a few minutes the glow was gone. There were clouds over the stars—the unfamiliar stars grouped in strange constellations—and the wind had a sharp rawness. The axis of Ryn too inclined toward its orbital plane, and it was the fall of the year.

The land felt big and empty as he walked. The mother land, he thought, the cradle of my race, and where are they all now? If there are Vanryn left here they are surely hiding. The skitter-planes have not been able to find that village yet, if it was a village. Are there other colonies across this broad island universe, other Ryn-type, Earth-type planets where the seed still flourishes? Or are we the last survivors?

Fairlie felt very lonely as he walked.

Christensen was sleeping when he got back to the ship. Fairlie had wanted to talk to him, not about anything in particular. Christensen, oddly enough, seemed to be the only one he could talk to about anything more than trivia. But he did not wake him. He had begun to fear that Christensen might be going to die, and the thought made him strangely sad, almost as though he would be losing a second father.

Everybody else, it seemed, was either sleeping or engrossed in work. Fairlie ate and then lay down on his own couch, far too restless and disturbed, he thought, to sleep, but he was physically weary from hours of hanging about the damned silly excavation and he wanted to rest.

He did not know that he had slept until he felt a shaking and roused up startled to see the face of the young flight-technician named Smith bent over him.

"Doctor Fairlie, DeWitt's on the walkie-talkie. He wants you right away."

Fairlie tried to force the cobwebs out of his brain. "Has he found something?" He swung his feet to the floor.

Smith's eyes were bright and his voice had a quality of high excitement.

"I don't know, but the way he spoke—I think something's found him."

Fairlie's solar plexus contracted with a great start, and adrenalin poured through him in a hot current. The cobwebs went. He gave Smith one look and then sprang toward the door, with the young man following closely.

In the communications room Fairlie picked up the field telephone and said, "Fairlie speaking. Over."

DeWitt's voice came crackling out of the ear-piece. He was almost incoherent. "—out there somewhere. One of the boys heard it—then me. I'm sure of it, Fairlie, but it's dark as the pits of hell out there, I want you. Get out here. I want you to talk to them, if they're there."

The line went dead.

Fairlie stood shivering. What was it—excitement, hope, fear, something more perhaps, something called dread? His teeth clacked together. Get out here, I want you to talk to them.

Yes. In the black dark among the old stones of the city. Talk to them.

Smith cleared his throat. "Doctor Fairlie. Sir. Uh—could I come with you?"

"You bet you can," said Fairlie. "You can do more than that. You can hold my hand all the way."

He left instructions for someone to be in the communications room every minute, literally and without fail. If Christensen awoke he was to be advised, but Fairlie could not see any reason to rouse him now.

"Wait and see if there is anything to report. It may be a false alarm—probably is."

DeWitt was both tired and obsessed. He could be seeing people

100

where there were only shadows, hearing them where there was only wind.

Fairlie went out of the ship with Smith.

They hurried. The night was very dark with clouds. The wind drove at them. From time to time a blurred splotch of purplish light appeared where one of the moons rode but its face was hidden. Smith carried a powerful flashlight. Its beam leaped and bobbled across the ground ahead of their feet. Fairlie had a wild desire to tell him to turn it off. It made them obvious, naked, unprotected in the dark. He fought down this desire, but his skin crawled and he peered around anxiously, seeing nothing, hearing nothing but the soft whisper of dry grass under the wind.

A thought was knocking at the back of his mind. He didn't want to let it in but it came anyway.

We haven't see any sign of the Vanryn. All we have seen is where they were destroyed. Maybe the enemy did annihilate them, maybe he moved in and took over the planet, it's perfectly possible, and maybe it's the enemy out there watching DeWitt, stalking among the stones, looking at the men who broke their law and took to the starways again. And we can't really say for sure that the enemy was human. We presume that they were, we do not believe in monsters, but we don't *know*.

Suddenly the horrid memories of the nightmare he had had aboard ship as they crossed the void of nothing between the stars returned to him. A feeling of power, Christensen had said, and the power is not human.

"Hey, Doctor!" Smith's voice startled him. "This way. There are the lights, over there."

Fairlie altered his course, toward the hard flare around the excavation. They picked their way precariously among the stones. A light moisture flicked suddenly across his face, flung by the wind. He shivered. Rain.

There was a comfort in the floodlights, the voices of the men, the prosaic machines. Nothing was working now. The men stood or sat close together, their eyes moving anxiously around the perimeter of vision. They blinked and shrugged deeper into their clothing as the thin rain swept at them. Fairlie could not see either DeWitt or Thomason.

"They're waiting for you," one of the men said. "Over there somewhere." He pointed. "That's where we heard it last."

"Just what did you hear?" Fairlie asked. The man had a blunt competent face, the kind of face that belongs with heavy machinery and matters of a concrete solidity. This was reassuring. The man had a frightened, uneasy look in his eyes. This was not reassuring.

"Voices," the man said. "At least that's what it sounded like, people talking, as though they didn't think they'd be overheard but the wind carried it. Then DeWitt began shouting and they shut up and we all listened real hard but you couldn't tell if it was people sneaking around or just the grass and bushes rustling in the wind." He wiped moisture off his face with a big grease-stained hand. "Now we're all hearing a whole damned army sneaking around out there." He looked at Fairlie. "I'm glad you're here."

I'm not, thought Fairlie. He stumbled around the heaped dirt with Smith. The brown soil was taking on a greasy shine. He moved farther and farther from the center of light, into a dimness of shadow and rain. He called DeWitt two or three times before he got an answer and made out the shapes of the two men sitting on a hump of rock hunched forward like two vultures on a tombstone.

"Where the hell have you been?" DeWitt said, getting up. He waved his arm at the night. "There's somebody out there. We know it, we all heard them. Call to them. Make them understand we're friends."

"I've told you before that in all this time the language will have changed," protested Fairlie. "Can't you see that? The chances of their understanding me are about nil."

"Don't give me scholarly obstructionism now," DeWitt said violently. "How do you know you won't get through to them? Go ahead. Try!"

Fairlie felt both irritated and nervous, it was almost hopeless,

102

but he moved a little distance more away from the light, into the shadow.

He called.

His throat was dry. His voice came out croaking and quavering and was lost in the wind.

"Hell," DeWitt said. "They couldn't hear you if they were standing next to you. Get out there. Go on." He swore. "What are you scared of? I'll come with you."

"I'm scared," Fairlie said. "And you know what you can do? You can—" It was his turn to swear. He turned and walked farther into the darkness and DeWitt came with him. Nobody told Smith to stay behind so he came too and Thomason followed behind him.

Fairlie called again.

"We are friends. Please speak to us." His tongue was stiff and awkward with the alien speech. He had difficulty remembering the words he had heard spoken so many times from the silvery spheres and the tapes. "Long ago some of the Vanryn left this world and made a colony far away across space. We're the descendants of those Vanryn, come back to Ryn. Do you understand?"

The wind mocked him. Skifting rain danced over the ancient stones, grass and bushes shook, whispering. The night was full of sound and movement.

There.

A footfall, swift and furtive.

There.

The stooping run of a body through wet leaves.

There—!

No. Nothing.

The light rain stopped. A dull, dim, purple gleam of moonlight came through the clouds. It did not make the night much brighter, but even that little was better than nothing. They strained their eyes.

Dark plain. Black scattered clumps of ruin, grass, brush.

Nothing.

"Try again," DeWitt said fiercely, and shoved Fairlie onward. "Try again."

"Please!" shouted Fairlie into the dark wind. "We must speak with you, it's important for both of us. Please show yourselves. We come in peace."

DeWitt caught at his arm. "What's that?"

They froze, listening. And suddenly Fairlie knew that someone was there, hidden, watching—knew it as plainly as though he saw them.

"Please understand!" he shouted. "We are your own kin, part of your own history, come back—"

This time there was no doubt. From out of the dark plain there came a sound of laughter.

Forgetting his fear, Fairlie ran toward it.

"Where are you? Please come out."

More laughter. Light, mocking laughter, one voice, no, two voices, perfectly human. The wind broke the sound, tossed it here and there. Fairlie went among the stones, turning now this way, now that, pleading, calling.

In the dim purple glow something moved. It ran swift and stooping from one shadowed hump of ruin to another.

Fairlie chased it.

He ran with all his might. Laughter followed him. Now he was angry and he ran faster toward the hump his eye had marked. It was far away from any other shelter and if the person behind it ran again he would see him even in this abominable light.

Nothing stirred. Fairlie ran toward the hump, stretching out his hands.

A creeper caught his ankle and threw him heavily to the wet ground. He heard somebody move close by. Desperately he cried, "Don't run!" and struggled to his knees.

He stopped there.

He was looking into a face. The dull purple light showed it only as a paler smudge against the darkness, but even so Fairlie got an impression of beauty.

Even so, he knew it was the face of a woman.

104

16

WITHOUT THINKING about it at all, Fairlie reached and grabbed for the woman before she could run past him. He had been floundering through the dark, hunting and calling, and only laughter had mocked his search, and sheer desperation that she might get away dictated his sudden impulse. His hand closed on her forearm.

She struggled, trying to pull away from his grip. He held on, and scrambled to his feet, and just then the errant light in Smith's hand angled across the dark and caught her face.

A young face, with clear pale skin, a lovely modelling of bone and flesh, eyes of a very deep blue, dark hair with the rain-mist caught in it, a mouth made for enjoyment, for laughter. Before Fairlie could see any more the light shifted, flicking here and there as Smith came bounding toward them shouting, "There they are!"

"Listen," said Fairlie earnestly in the old Vanryn tongue. "We won't harm you. We are friends."

The shifting beam caught her figure and he saw that she wore a kind of hooded cloak against the night wind and the rain.

"Then let me go!" she said.

The words, the fact that he understood the words, hit Fairlie like a blow. It had seemed so utterly improbable that the old Vanryn language could still be understood or spoken here, that he could only stare at her. Had Kalber himself stood living before him, he would have been little more surprised.

His mind sought an explanation. Somehow, something had fixed the old Vanryn tongue so that it had not greatly changed in all this time. What had done that? He couldn't guess, but it had happened, and he had been understood by this woman of the Vanryn.

Woman of the Vanryn . . . The linguistic problem faded from his thoughts as the full impact of the strangeness of all this reached him.

Voices on a record, shadows dead and dust for ages, guesses, conjectures, ghosts—no more. But she is of the Vanryn, none the less. She stands erect and living before me, watching me with intelligent eyes, thinking God knows what thoughts about me, and she is real.

The same stock. The same flesh, blood, genes, and chromosomes. My brothers of Altair.

Good Lord, he thought. Oh, good Lord.

The wind suddenly felt cold on him.

"By God, you've got one of them," DeWitt said, panting, his feet thumping on the ground as he ran up. "Good. Hold the light steady, Smith. I want to see what they look like."

Smith held the light steady.

Very irritably Fairlie said in English, "I wasn't trying to take her prisoner, I just wanted to talk to her. She can understand me."

"And you were so sure that was impossible!" said DeWitt. He peered at the woman for a long time, his eyes shining bright and hard, his mouth stretched in a grin of nervous excitement. "All right, fine. Go ahead. Talk to her. Ask her how many of them are here. Ask what they're doing here, if they were sent to spy on us. Ask her where the rest of her people are, and what cities they have, what ships, what machines."

Fairlie, still feeling a bit numb, asked her.

"Machines?" said the woman. It was as though the word that Fairlie used, the old word that the Vanryn of the past had known

106

perfectly well, was a little strange to her. She said after a moment, "We have nothing like that. Nothing."

"What does she say?" DeWitt demanded impatiently. And when Fairlie translated, his face got harsh. "She's hiding something. These people belong to the Vanryn, or she wouldn't know and speak their language. You ask her again."

Fairlie disregarded him and said earnestly to the woman, "Listen. We want to be your friends. We've come a long way to Ryn."

She said, "In the ship that we saw and heard?"

"So you do know something about ships," Fairlie said eagerly, "Yet you say you have none?"

She shook her head. "We do not. That is why Thrayn—that is why we—were curious."

"Who is Thrayn?"

Her eyes mocked him. "Thrayn is Thrayn. And I am Aral."

DeWitt broke in roughly. "Fairlie, this isn't a private chat, I want an interpretation as we go along."

Fairlie translated, and DeWitt said disgustedly, "You're getting nowhere. She's covering up. We didn't come here to—"

He broke off as Thomason came stumbling to join them. DeWitt cut short Thomason's ejaculation of astonishment. "Yes, we got one but there's more around here somewhere. You and Smith have a look around. I'll take the light. Hurry!"

The woman Aral was looking at DeWitt's hard face and she turned and said ironically to Fairlie, "He is my friend too?"

"He's only one officer of our scientific expedition," said Fairlie quickly. "He's not our commander. He won't—" He stopped. He had been going to say, "He won't hurt you," but he found that he couldn't say that. Looking at DeWitt, at the excitement and harsh purpose in his face, he was not sure of that. To shortcut things, DeWitt might be ruthless.

Fairlie turned back to the woman and said, "Aral, if I let you go now will you come back? With more of your people? To meet us as friends?"

Her eyes narrowed quickly, and she said, "Yes."

107

"Then go."

He released his hold on her forearm and she turned and went away like a bird. DeWitt uttered a yell of surprise and anger and grabbed for her but he missed her and stumbled, and the light dropped from his hand as he went momentarily to his knees.

Her voice called in the darkness, high and silvery. "Thrayn!"

Then there was nothing, and Fairlie stood looking into the purple-shot darkness without seeing anything.

"I ought to throttle you!" DeWitt said furiously. "You deliberately let her go!"

"I let her go," said Fairlie. "Yes. I told you I hadn't taken her prisoner. Christensen gave us clear orders on how to deal with any people here."

"Christensen be damned," said DeWitt. Fairlie thought the man was coming at him. But then Thomason and Smith came running back.

"I saw her—just a glimpse," said Smith. He pointed. "Running that way. There was another one with her. A man, I think."

"We'll never catch them in the dark," said Thomason. "What happened?"

DeWitt did not answer that. His face was still dark and tight but he seemed to have got a hold on his anger. "You might as well get the work going again," he said to Thomason. "I'm going back to the ship."

Fairlie said, "I'm going with you."

DeWitt looked at him. "Sure."

Smith had picked up the light from where DeWitt had dropped it. "She sure was pretty," he said, and shook his head smiling.

DeWitt snapped, "Bring the light." He set off.

Fairlie marched behind him. Smith looked at Thomason, gave a puzzled shrug, and followed with the flashlight.

DeWitt paused long enough at the excavation to fling an order at the man with the walkie-talkie. Then he strode on toward the ship. Nobody spoke as they trudged grimly. And as Fairlie's outrage abated he began to think more clearly and he could see

108

trouble approaching critical mass, getting closer to it with every stride DeWitt took.

Fairlie thought of the woman out there in the dark night. He wondered what she was thinking, what she was saying to her companion, what they were doing. He wondered if they would ever come back, if he would ever see Aral again. Whether or no, the contact had been made, the thing was done. It would have some kind of an impact on the Vanryn, wherever they were and however they lived. Thirty centuries of history had caught up with them, and that was not a thing that could be overlooked.

He watched DeWitt striding hard ahead of him. He didn't think that they would be allowed to overlook it.

It was raining again when they reached the ship, real drops this time that tapped and rattled on the metal wall around the hatch. It was a homely, Earthly sound and it suddenly wrenched at Fairlie's heart. He yearned to be back there. He yearned never to have come. This nighted world seemed abruptly to become nightmarishly strange.

DeWitt stamped away down the corridor ahead of him, and even his back looked dangerous.

Christensen was waiting in the lounge with Raab and Winstedt. He looked quickly from DeWitt to Fairlie and back again.

"What happened?"

"Ask Sir Galahad here," said DeWitt savagely. "We had one of them but she was female and good-looking and Fairlie let her go. We didn't get more than a dozen words out of her, and all of them were lies."

"I don't go along with DeWitt's methods," said Fairlie stiffly, when Christensen turned to him. "I don't believe that taking these people prisoner and then browbeating them is any way to establish relations."

Fairlie looked at DeWitt. "If you hadn't come charging in I could have talked to her, made her understand we were friends. But she knew damn well you weren't friendly."

"If she wasn't hiding something, what was she scared of?" said DeWitt contemptuously.

109

"Just a minute," said Christensen. "I thought all that had been made quite clear to you, DeWitt. I'm thankful Fairlie had the sense to let her go." He was very angry. He turned and glared at Fairlie. "Why didn't you let me know what was going on? I should have been out there myself. Then this wouldn't have happened. Well, you talked to her. What did she say? What did she tell you?"

"That her people know nothing about machines or ships or things like that. That was as much as I got out of her before DeWitt started to get rough."

"She lied," DeWitt said. "She knew what a ship was, from what you said yourself. These people are no dumb savages. I got a good look at that girl. Aside from being pretty she was civilized. Everything about her showed it. She was clean and she was soft. You don't find either of those qualities much in a primitive society."

He looked past Christensen, appealing to Winstedt, to Raab.

"These people must have cities somewhere. And they could tell us a lot about what we're after. That's what the expedition came for, wasn't it? Are we supposed to go home—and that's kind of a long way—empty-handed because we're too polite to ask the natives a simple question? Or because somebody's afraid they might answer it?"

He was talking fast, talking hard, not giving Christensen a chance to break in.

"There were at least two of these Vanryn out there, and they can't have come from too far away. They didn't come in any ground or air vehicle or we'd have heard them going away, let alone our radar-watch would have caught it. They might have some kind of a riding-animal but I doubt it, there hasn't been any sign of an animal that big. So I think they came on foot, and that means the rest of them aren't far from here. I think we ought to get the hell out and look for them."

"What would you propose doing when you found them?" asked Winstedt. "Supposing they didn't want to come back."

"I think they could be persuaded," DeWitt said, "to lead us to wherever they came from."

Christensen broke in. "Possibly they could. But do you think it would be wise?"

DeWitt looked at him narrowly. "I think you worry too much about wisdom."

"You don't worry enough. How many men would you need for this expedition to their supposed city? Half, three-quarters of our force?"

"At least that. We'd want a strong party just in case."

Now Christensen turned to Raab and Winstedt. "That would leave this ship virtually unprotected. And if another ship came from Earth, a ship of our enemies, we could be completely destroyed."

"We certainly can't risk that," said Winstedt, worriedly.

Raab nodded. "Our findings here are too vital. You know that, DeWitt. We can't allow the other side to—"

"Risk!" said DeWitt. "I tell you there isn't any risk of a ship of enemies getting here from Earth. The important thing is to find those people, find their city, find what we came for."

A curious expression came into Christensen's face, and he spoke in a soft voice.

"So there isn't any risk. That's interesting. I had thought all along this was a race against time, a race to get ahead of the enemy. I thought they were busy building a ship which would come close after us. But all along I've had a hunch on this, and your indifference about taking defensive measures after we landed, strengthened it. And now I know."

DeWitt started to speak but Christensen's voice rang hard and clear, drowning him out. He said, "You know there isn't any danger because you know our enemies *can't* build a ship. They never heard of the Vanryn. They never had the slightest idea of what we found at Gassendi."

"But my tapes," said Fairlie. "The tapes and translations that the spy stole from me!"

111

Christensen said, "There wasn't any spy. That was all a scare, a hoax."

"What do you mean? Somebody *did* knock me out."

Christensen looked at DeWitt. "Yes, Fairlie, somebody did. DeWitt did."

17

FAIRLIE STARED at Christensen, feeling as stunned as he had on that night when the lights went out and the unseen assailant struck him from behind. He was aware of a tight, hard silence. He turned to look at DeWitt, but he could read nothing in the man's face.

Winstedt said, "Is that true?"

DeWitt shrugged. "Christensen made the accusation. Let him prove it."

"I can't prove it," Christensen said. "There is no proof, nothing I could bring up then to my superiors, nothing even now that would hold up in a court of law. But I know."

Winstedt's round pursy cheeks were pale. "That is a very serious accusation, Christensen. I can't believe it. Why would he do such a thing?"

"Do you want to tell them, DeWitt, or shall I?"

"You seem to be doing all the talking. Go ahead."

"All right. You wanted this ship to be built, you wanted this voyage to be made. You were being balked by those you called obstructionists and cowards, and you began to be afraid that the whole business might be held off indefinitely, perhaps for years. You were afraid you might lose it. So you decided to force the issue. If we thought the other side was in on it too, if we thought our enemies had stolen our secret, then we couldn't afford to wait. A simple matter of rapping Fairlie on the head and stealing

113

his tapes, and we'd get the project going in a hurry. No wonder Security could never turn up the slightest evidence of a spy on the base."

Raab studied DeWitt with cool interest. "That has a quality of logic."

"Yes," said Fairlie. "It does."

Rip and tear, stop at nothing, make things go the way you want them to. He could see DeWitt quite calmly cutting the power line and then proceeding to the rest of the task with brisk efficiency. The brief wait, the quick blow, the unconcerned step over the prostrate body, the swift but careful rifling of the lab, and never once anywhere along the line one smallest single doubt, one qualm of conscience.

Winstedt began, "I hardly know what to say."

"Make your usual speech," said DeWitt. "The one that takes no sides and makes no enemies." He looked around them contemptuously. "What happened all that time ago on Earth isn't important. What is here is important, and we're wasting time. The Vanryn—"

"—are going to be left alone," said Christensen. "They're not obligated to tell you anything, DeWitt. You keep you hands off them. Keep them off, do you hear? You make me sick, DeWitt. You're a stupid, narrow-minded man, a dangerous man, a fanatic. What happened there on Earth *is* important, as a measure of what you're capable of doing. You don't—"

His voice faltered. A sudden gray pallor had come over his face. "You don't have any balance," he said, and then put out his hand toward Fairlie. "I think I—"

Fairlie caught him as he fell. Gaunt as he was he was still heavy, more than Fairlie could handle. Winstedt stepped in to help.

"I'll go for Reicher," Raab said, and left.

Between them, Winstedt and Fairlie lifted Christensen onto a couch. His breathing was labored. Fairlie opened his shirt. Christensen's eyes were open but Fairlie could not tell how much he saw or understood. He kept telling him to take it easy, every-

114

thing was all right. Reicher came. Fairlie stepped back to give him room and saw that DeWitt was no longer there.

That was a very long night.

Reicher worked over Christensen a while. Then he had him carried to the minute sickbay, where he worked over him some more. When Christensen slept, Fairlie, Winstedt, and Raab took turns watching. Reicher refused to say how bad it was. He didn't know yet. But Fairlie thought it was bad enough.

DeWitt did not come near the sickbay until nearly dawn. Then he glanced in only for a moment and was gone again. Fairlie got the impression that DeWitt was hurrying to get something done before Christensen could come round and stop him. He considered trying to stop DeWitt himself and gave it up because it was manifestly impossible. DeWitt was subordinate only to Christensen and Fairlie was subordinate to practically everybody.

There was nothing to do but wait.

Fairlie slept a little. Sometime around daybreak Raab woke him. "Christensen wants you. And me, but not Winstedt. I don't know why."

When they came into the sickbay Reicher said, "Don't stay long." He went out and Christensen looked up at them. His glance was clear now and when he spoke his voice was weak but normal.

He did not waste any time.

"Reicher won't tell me how long I've got, but it doesn't matter as far as the expedition is concerned. I can't hold active command any longer. DeWitt knows it. He'll take over."

He stopped to rest, as though even that small effort had tired him. Fairlie stood waiting. He wanted to do something he had not done since he was a child. He wanted to cry.

Christensen said, "I want you two to try and act in my place. Raab because he has no personal passions to be served, Fairlie because he thinks the way I do."

"But—" said Fairlie.

"—have to do the best you can. DeWitt needs a check on him, try to hold him down. I can't give you any real authority because

115

I can't enforce it, but you've got to try. If he finds weapons, power—"

Again the wait, the slow hard breathing.

"He's a danger, that man. Try to hold him down."

Fairlie started again to say something but Reicher appeared in the doorway motioning them to leave.

Outside in the corridor Raab said, "I wish he had not said that."

Fairlie shook his head, dismayed.

"I have more important things to do," Raab said, "than worry about DeWitt. Still—"

They walked slowly down the corridor side by side, brooding.

A mess, thought Fairlie. A real mess. Christensen is a born leader and I'm not, I can have my human angers and I can kick back when I get kicked, but I can see myself trying to tell DeWitt what to do and nothing to back me up but Christensen said—

"Still it's possible that Christensen is right," said Raab. "DeWitt is a type. I've met it before, in science, in teaching, in politics, and it is a dangerous type, more dangerous than the self-seeking and flexible scoundrel. These men are honest and they're loyal. They see a job before them and they're convinced that their world depends upon the doing of that job come hell or high water. Every other consideration including reason and common sense goes out the window. This could mean disaster for all of us right here and now. If these Vanryn do indeed have weapons and if they are sufficiently provoked—"

"Yes," said Fairlie. He felt very tired and at least a hundred years old. "I guess I'd better go find DeWitt."

He was not inside the ship.

"He sent the skitter-planes out at the crack of dawn," said the man in the Communications room. "One of 'em just called in a few minutes ago—pilot said he'd spotted something. He was going to make sure and then come back. DeWitt went out of here so fast you could hear thunder. I expect he's waiting for the 'copter."

Fairlie went outside. He stood for a moment, dazzled by the yellowish-diamond glare of rising Altair. The early morning sky

116

was pale brass, not copper yet. The scintillating blaze of it flooded the world, and dark and big against that sky stood DeWitt, his back to the ship, peering toward the distant forest.

DeWitt turned when Fairlie came up to him. He said curtly, "I'm now officially in command."

"I've heard," said Fairlie.

DeWitt looked at him. "What did Christensen tell you?" And then before Fairlie could answer, DeWitt uttered a snorting sound. "I can imagine. He was trying to set you and Raab against me, wasn't he? Listen, Fairlie. You're under my orders now. You remember that."

Fairlie had always thought that silence was the best way when you were dealing with belligerence. Don't lose your calmness, your detachment, stay cool and refuse to descend to brawling.

That was what he had always thought. But now something surprised him, something hot and furious that came up inside him and would not be silenced.

"I didn't ask in on all this, DeWitt," he said savagely, "I was pulled into it without my knowledge or consent, if you remember. You needed me, and you gave me no say about it. All right—"

He felt himself trembling a little in his anger and that was a feeling he had had too often in these last hours.

"All right. I did what you wanted me to do, I cracked the Vanryn language. More by luck than skill, I'll admit. But I did it. If I hadn't you wouldn't be here, none of us would. Christensen aside, I feel a responsibility about all this, and I am *not* a corporal being ordered around by a colonel."

He was shaking with anger and he thought that he must present a slightly ridiculous figure but DeWitt did not seem to find him so. DeWitt gave him a hard look, a coldly appraising look. Then he turned abruptly around and away from Fairlie, as the drone of a motor came through the sunrise.

The helicopter came in low over the distant forest, like an ungainly bird. It touched down and the pilot—it was young Smith, the rocket flight-technician, doing another of his multiple jobs—came toward them fast.

117

"Well?" said DeWitt.

Smith nodded vigorously. "I spotted them. A man and a woman, heading northeast. Can't be any doubt it's the same ones."

A man and a woman. Thrayn and Aral. And Fairlie could see again the finely modelled face and hear the silvery voice that was so like the voice of the long-dead woman who had sung to stars.

"They took cover the minute they saw me, but a little too late," Smith was saying. "I charted their location, and then used the auto-mapping cameras on the way back."

"Thank God somebody knows his job," grunted DeWitt. "Let's get those maps processed fast."

Later, in the ship, Fairlie looked with the others at the photo-maps that had been pieced together and lay on a table, a slightly fuzzy panorama of forest and hill and mountain. A long, sharp black arrow had been drawn across the fuzziness, pointing away from the blank black place that was the plain of the ship.

An arrow pointing to—what? Fairlie wondered.

DeWitt spoke crisply. He had a look of tough confidence now, he was born to be a leader and finally after all the years of frustration he had got the reins of leadership into his hands.

"The Vanryn—some of them, at least—are out there some-where." His brown hand smacked the map where the arrow pointed. "That man and woman are walking so it can't be too far."

Thomason frowned. "There's nothing like a city showing on these photos."

"Which only means it must be a little beyond the area that Smith mapped," DeWitt said. "But it can't be too far beyond. And we're going to find it." His eyes swept their faces. "We'll go in two tracs, and the other two can go along with us the first couple of days to carry extra fuel. Personnel—Raab, Fairlie, Winstedt, Smith, Hagulian and two drivers, beside myself, in the advance party. Thomason will command here in my absence."

Thomason nodded without enthusiasm and asked, "What about weapons?"

118

"Damn little," DeWitt said. "There wouldn't have been any, if Christensen had had his way. But I managed to smuggle a few guns and a few hundred rounds aboard."

Raab said, "I'd like to be explicit. What, exactly, is our party after?"

"I'll tell you, exactly," said DeWitt in a flat voice. "We're after what we found in Gassendi, only more. We're after any Vanryn technologies and artifacts that can make our country strong against its enemies, before those enemies destroy us. Is that explicit enough?"

Nobody made any answer. DeWitt added, "We are *not* after abstruse scientific data, measurements of magnetic field, interesting geological theories, and the sort of thing that would make fine prestige papers at the next convention of the Association for the Advancement of Science. All that can come later."

Raab was not at all crushed. He said, "This talk of guns—I protest that that's the worst possible way to learn things from people."

"Oh, Christ, do you suppose I don't know that," DeWitt snapped. "Give me credit for a little sense. The guns, and damn few of them there are, are for Thomason's protection here." He looked at his watch. "I suggest that we get busy. I expect to get under way tomorrow, early."

Before dawn on the next day, Fairlie slipped quietly into Christensen's cabin. Christensen was sleeping, and it seemed to Fairlie that he looked a little better. Reicher was sitting beside the bunk.

"We're starting," Fairlie said. "I thought maybe he'd be awake."

Reicher shook his head. "No, I'm keeping him under sedation. His heart's somewhat better, though."

"Good."

"Yes, it is."

And that was that, thought Fairlie, and he went back out and picked up his pack. He felt a little cheered, but not much. He wished Christensen had been awake.

Out in the pre-dawn darkness, the wind blew cold and damp. There were lights going and the tracs were being loaded up. One of them roared and shook as its driver tested the motor. Winstedt went by him, podgier than ever in a short coat, his round face unhappy.

Why, Fairlie wondered, did he feel a little thrill of anticipation in spite of his forebodings? He thought he knew why.

The woman Aral. She was out there somewhere and he was going to see her again. And somehow her mocking face and her silver voice had got mixed up in his mind with that other woman of long ago, the woman whose song to the stars was on one of the tapes in his pack. Yes. He wanted to see Aral again.

DeWitt's voice cut through his thoughts, and he looked and saw DeWitt over by the lights, speaking to the trac-drivers harshly.

"You've got six minutes to load the rest of it. No more."

Again, he loomed up dark and bigger than life against the lights, and Fairlie had a hopeless premonition that DeWitt was too big to fight against, that he would drive ahead despite anything Fairlie and Raab could do; and that he would succeed, and in success take war out of the little theater of Earth and spread it clear across the stars that were still haunted by that struggle of long ago.

18

THEY HAD BEEN moving through the forest for three days, and the going had been easy. Too easy, Fairlie thought.

Winstedt echoed his thought aloud. Tenderly shifting his plump backside on the hard, narrow seat of the trac, he said, "I never expected this. It isn't natural."

DeWitt turned from his seat beside the driver. "What isn't?"

Winstedt swept his pink hand around in a wide gesture. "This forest. It isn't natural forest at all, it's park. But park that nobody cares for."

The sky had been heavily clouded ever since they started, and still was. And the clouds were the color of verdigris, so that the heavy light that poured down through them was tinged with a poisonous, green-yellow color. It would have made any place look queer, Fairlie thought, and this forest was queer enough to begin with. No, not forest, Winstedt was right about that, this was not like any Earthly forest.

There were trees. Big trees, medium-sized ones, small ones. Most of them were deciduous and in this fall season green leaves and rotted no-color leaves formed a mat on the ground. You looked at them and you thought that it was not too much different from Earth. But the second and third and fiftieth time you looked, it became more and more strange.

The leaves that had dropped from some of the trees had not changed color. That was a small thing but it bothered Fairlie.

121

Leaves should change color before they fell, but these had not. Furthermore, there were some trees that still had bright green leaves on them, and some of the smaller trees had fruits on them, odd-looking big purple and orange and yellow fruits like swollen pods. There had been quite a blow-up over those fruits the first day out. Hagulian, the irrepressible young geologist, had been caught sampling them and Winstedt had squeaked warnings and DeWitt had given Hagulian a savage dressing-down. Yet so far, Hagulian had not been sick.

Trees, leaves and fruits beneath the sullen verdigris sky, and yet it was not a forest. There were no animals of size. Birds were few, and silent. More surprising yet, there was almost no underbrush between the smooth boles of the trees, no clogging vines and creepers, no thickets of thorn and briar. In that respect, Winstedt was quite right. It looked like a vast park.

"It's as though the common parasitic plants never developed here at all," Winstedt said, as the trac rolled down a shadowed, sloping glade.

"Maybe they were got rid of," said DeWitt.

Winstedt stared at him, a little vacantly. "Got rid of?"

"I should think," said DeWitt, "that a people who could fly the stars could have cleaned up their own world easily enough."

Fairlie had been looking back at the other trac, following them a hundred yards behind. Besides its driver, Hagulian was in it, and young Smith, and Raab. It was no accident, he was thinking, that he and Raab did not ride together. He turned again in his seat when DeWitt said that.

Fairlie said satirically, "The Vanryn, the super-scientists, is that it? The same ones who make those trails?"

They had found trails in the forest, old and narrow and worn deeply into the ground.

"Those trails don't prove a thing," DeWitt said.

"They're foot-trails, for all the world like Indian trails," prodded Fairlie. "Super-scientists wouldn't be out footing it through the woods, would they?"

DeWitt made no answer to that, but his back was as uncompromising as a rock as he stared ahead. The tracs rolled on down the easy slope, came to a shallow stream and forded it, and went on.

The sullen sky became duskier, and the damp air turned chill. In a grove of towering, shining boles whose foliage was so high above them that it was like a cathedral roof, DeWitt made the sign to halt for the night.

DeWitt studied the photo-maps while the rest of them sat around on the short grass and ate their rations. Hagulian looked longingly at a few of the small trees nearby that had big yellow fruit-pods on them.

"No," said Winstedt emphatically.

"It didn't hurt me," said Hagulian. "Not a bit. And it was *good*."

"For all you know, you're crawling with unknown viruses right now," said Winstedt.

Muirhead, who drove Trac One, a lanky, mild-eyed, dreamy-looking young man, shivered a little as the damp wind blew more strongly through the glade. He said, "If I were back home in California, I'd say that the rains were coming on."

Fairlie nodded. "I've heard you have quite a rainy season out there—I never got out to the Coast, myself."

All of a sudden, the ludicrousness of that sober remark struck him. He had been, unconsciously, thinking of California as a long way off, clear across the country. They had come through vast nothingness to Ryn, to the third world of Altair, but they could not leave familiar habits of thought behind them.

DeWitt, with the photo-maps spread across his knees, talked without looking up at them.

"We'll base here temporarily and search till we find them. If we can't locate any Vanryn community, I'll call Thomason and have him send the skitter-planes to help. They must be some-where in this area."

"And if they're not?" asked Raab.

DeWitt said, "We'll keep looking."

Fairlie felt depressed. The sky had darkened until its cloud-cover was the color of corroded brass. The faces of the others had an odd look in that light. He was sick of their faces. He was tired of this whole expedition and he didn't give a damn if they never found the Vanryn. As soon as it was dark, he rolled up in his sleeping-bag.

Next morning the clouds persisted and the wind blew cooler and damper. They were morosely eating their breakfast out of tins when Muirhead suddenly dropped his tin. He said, incoherently, "Hey, look. Hey, look there—"

The men started scrambling to their feet. Fairlie couldn't see what had startled them but he got up and looked past Muirhead and then he saw.

A hundred feet away in the dusky grove stood a man, looking at them.

Fairlie's heart bounded painfully. Nobody said anything, they all just stood there looking. The man did not speak or move either. He was dark-haired, with golden-tan skin, and he wore a short tunic of dark green and sandals and nothing else.

DeWitt's voice suddenly crackled behind them. "Now listen, don't scare him off! Sit down and go on eating. You hear me—sit down!"

The men started to sit down but did so awkwardly, not taking their eyes off the motionless figure there in the dusky shadows. DeWitt came and grabbed Fairlie by the arm.

"All right, Fairlie, here's where you do your stuff, and I want it done better than last time. Go on out to him. Tell him we just came on a friendly visit. Ask him to come into camp."

Fairlie stood his ground. "I want your word first that if he does he'll be unharmed."

"All right, you have it," snapped DeWitt. "Now stop gabbling and get out there before he runs away."

Fairlie started walking out toward the man. He saw the man come to a more alert posture, and he shouted to him, in the old Vanryn, "I come in friendship."

He was near enough now that he could see the man's face.

This was a young man, dark and handsome and strong-looking, with intelligent eyes.

Fairlie judged it best to stop ten feet away from him. They looked at each other with mingled curiosity and wariness.

Fairlie thought, What the devil, this is an historic moment and all we can do is stand here and gawk at each other.

He was going to repeat his protestation of friendship when the other spoke, briefly and rapidly. Fairlie could not understand, and said so. The man repeated more slowly, and this time Fairlie got the meaning.

"Why have you followed us?"

"Followed you?" said Fairlie. Then he began to comprehend. He said, "You are Thrayn?"

"I am Thrayn."

"The woman, Aral, was with you the other night in the ruins."

Thrayn nodded curtly. "She is with me now." He glanced sidewise.

Fairlie, looking that way, saw the woman standing farther back in the grove, beside a big tree whose massive trunk sheltered her in deeper shadow.

She did not wear a cloak now. She wore a tunic like Thrayn's, except that it was a paler green in color. Her dark hair was bare and so were her arms and legs. She looked gravely and doubtfully at Fairlie from a distance, and said nothing.

"Try to understand," said Fairlie. "We come from a very far star and world, but we are your kinsmen. Perhaps you still have memory of the time when the Vanryn conquered the stars?"

Thrayn said soberly, "We have that memory." He looked steadily at Fairlie and then he said, "You say you are our friends, you wish us well?"

"Yes."

"Then go away."

"But why?" Fairlie protested. "We came here only to learn, we will harm no one."

"My people," Thrayn said slowly, "are afraid. And they are very angry with me and with Aral because our curiosity about

125

your ship has now led you this way. They have made us come out to meet you, to tell you to leave Ryn."

"They've no reason to be afraid of us—" Fairlie began.

But Thrayn interrupted. "It is not you they fear. It is the Llorn."

The name rang and echoed like a bell-note in the momentary silence that followed. Fairlie stared and then, uncomprehendingly, repeated it. "The Llorn?"

"There was a war long ago," Thrayn said earnestly. "It was fought across the stars. And our ancestors lost that war."

Now, Fairlie began to understand. "And the name of your enemies was, the Llorn?"

Thrayn nodded. "Yes. They were very powerful, more powerful even than the Vanryn. They forced us back to Ryn. They destroyed our starport and our ships. And before they left they warned that if ever the Vanryn flew space again, total destruction would follow. That is why my people are afraid. Because a ship has come to Ryn and the prohibition of the Llorn has been broken."

"But that was many ages ago," Fairlie protested. "Surely you don't believe that the Llorn are any danger now?"

He saw a change in Thrayn's face, a shade of indecision.

"*Do* you believe it?" Fairlie pressed.

"I don't know," Thrayn admitted, finally. "I have thought sometimes that we have allowed an old legend to cramp and stifle us." A deep spark came into his eyes as he spoke. "I have seen the Hall of Suns, I have dreamed of the ships of old. I—" He broke off.

Fairlie thought he understood. A dreamer, a rebel against the ancient tradition of fear that still haunted his people. He guessed now what impulse had made Thrayn come to peer at the ship. He spoke to Thrayn, loudly enough so that the woman could also hear him.

"We were surprised and excited before, when we met you in the dark. But we are friends, and want to discuss this thing with

126

you. Will you come into our camp? Again I say, you can go when you please."

Thrayn looked thoughtfully at the men and the two tracs under the distant trees, and then he turned and looked questioningly at Aral.

Aral, after a moment, walked forward to Thrayn's side. Unexpectedly, she laughed, a ripple of silver, as she looked at Fairlie. Her dark eyes were confident now and a little mocking.

"Let us go, Thrayn," she said. "He will not let them harm *me*."

Fairlie flushed and felt like a fool. Did his admiration for the woman show that clearly?

She started forward, and so did Thrayn, and Fairlie walked beside them back to where DeWitt stood waiting in front of the other staring men. DeWitt's face wore a pleasant smile but the glitter in his eyes showed his excitement.

One of the men, Fairlie thought it was Hagulian, uttered a long low whistle as Aral came closer.

Still smiling and without turning his head, DeWitt said softly, "I want to tell you right now, that if any of you makes any woman-trouble here and queers things, I'll kill him."

He meant it, and they all knew it. There were no more whistles.

They came up to DeWitt and stopped, and DeWitt looked at them almost raptly. Then his expression changed.

Fairlie knew what it was. DeWitt was looking at the simple tunics that Thrayn and Aral wore. The cloth was heavy, roughly woven. And their sandals were of wood with woven thongs.

Thrayn said to Fairlie, "Tell them. Tell them that my people don't want them in their city."

DeWitt's eyes flared bright when he heard that. "City, eh? Now we're getting somewhere. Ask him where it is. Ask him if they have other cities."

Thrayn made a wide gesture in answer. "There are other cities of the Vanryn, yes. But they are far. Ours is near. And Aral and

I are sent to tell you that you must not come nearer to it."

Fairlie rapidly summarized what Thrayn had already said to him. But DeWitt smiled and shook his head.

"Oh, no, we're not going back after coming this far. Not because of a piece of ancient history. Say that we'll smooth it out with his people all right if he'll lead us to the city."

Thrayn looked troubled when he heard that. "I can't! My people have not thought of the Llorn for a long time, but now your coming has wakened old fears. They think you bring danger."

"There's no danger," DeWitt insisted. "He was curious about our ship, wasn't he? Tell him we'll take him to it later, and show it to him."

When Fairlie interpreted that, Thrayn's head came up with a curious pride and he said challengingly, "And what is your ship to the great ships of the Vanryn glory? To the ships that conquered a universe?"

"But that was long ago," Fairlie reminded. "Yet Vanryn ships might someday fly again, because of our coming to Ryn."

Thrayn seemed to struggle with indecision, and Fairlie felt a sympathy for the man. Aral stood silent. Finally Thrayn said, "I will take you, but I warn you again that I do not know how you will be met."

DeWitt grunted with satisfaction. "We'll take our chances there if he'll guide us. Tell him so. And ask him what the Llorn were like. We never did find out much about them."

Thrayn shrugged. "The legends are very old and timeworn. They speak of the 'shadow-wrapped ones,' the 'dark ones.'"

"Do they speak of the Llorn as human?" asked Fairlie.

"No."

19

THE SULLEN CLOUDED sky was becoming a dusky ocher when they stood on a low forested ridge and looked down at the Vanryn city.

A long way to come for this, thought Fairlie. *And I don't know whether to be glad or sorry.*

He did not look at DeWitt. He had come to hate DeWitt, and yet he did not want to see DeWitt's face in this moment of shattering disappointment.

There was a city down there, yes. It did not seem too big but it was hard to tell just how big it was because of the great trees that had grown up all through and over it, forming a perfect natural camouflage that explained why no aerial photograph had found this place. The streets of buildings under the great trees were not high ones but they were graceful in outline, their blockiness relieved by artfully soaring columns and buttresses. They could not be seen too clearly but they were dark and old and impressive in the yellow dusk.

Old. Not so old as the age-eaten ruins near the ship, but very old, very worn, crumbling around the edges. A column had fallen here, a façade was weathered and cracked there. From a few of them, a soft ruddy light like lamplight had begun to show, but whole streets and sections were dark and lightless.

Fairlie thought he could see a few moving figures in the shadowed streets but it was hard to see because of the trees. He also glimpsed, over at the side of the valley where the buildings ended, a large area clear of trees which held what looked like cultivated fields.

DeWitt said, in a flat expressionless tone, "Ask him if the other cities are like this."

Fairlie put the question. "Yes," said Thrayn. "Except for the old places that have fallen to ruin."

There was a little silence when Fairlie translated that, and they looked at each other, all except DeWitt.

Winstedt sighed heavily. "So this is what there is. And the great Vanryn are people raising turnips or whatever and living in places like this. That's fine."

DeWitt turned fiercely. "You give up mighty easily. We knew from our first look at it that things had slipped back on this world. It's the really old places, the places that could have the old Vanryn secrets in them, that we're after. You shut up, Winstedt."

He turned back to Fairlie and Thrayn. "We've come here to be friends. I want him to tell his people so. Give them a little warning, before we go down there."

Thrayn said, doubtfully, "I will tell them." He went down the dusking slope and Aral went with him, glancing back at Fairlie with a curiously intimate look, and then skipping along after Thrayn, her fine bare legs flashing.

Fairlie told himself that Aral was the most beautiful woman he had ever seen. He had talked with her on the way in the preceding hours. He had asked her if she and Thrayn were husband and wife.

She had laughed. "Not yet. Perhaps, indeed, we shall never be. But Thrayn interests me, he is different from our other men, with his dreams of the old Vanryn glory." She had added calmly, "And you interest me."

Fairlie's heart had skipped a beat, but he had asked dryly, "I in particular, or all of us strangers?"

She shrugged. "I can't talk with the others. You."

130

That was fine, Fairlie thought as he looked after her now, and what would Thrayn think of it if he knew?

The men hunkered down on the grass and began to eat their rations. They did not talk much but looked frequently down into the darkening valley.

DeWitt stood with his back to them, a dark immobile figure on the edge of the crest, waiting. The wind blew damp and cool and spiritless. DeWitt waited there until Thrayn came back up the slope, alone.

"Well?" asked DeWitt.

Thrayn's face was long, and he spoke directly to Fairlie. "They will not have you enter the city. They say you must go back to your ship and leave."

"And if we don't?"

"They did not say. But there is fear and there is anger."

"Will they attack us?"

"I don't know," said Thrayn. "They are very angry with me, and will not talk much with me. They think it is my fault you came here."

Fairlie translated. DeWitt stood silent for a moment. Then he said, "We won't try to force our way in there—we'll camp here and wait. They'll get used to us soon, and get over their superstitious nervousness."

When Thrayn heard that decision, he did not look too happy. He said, "I think you had better keep good watch." He turned and went away into the dark.

DeWitt brusquely told the others. He concluded, "I'll set watches. No guns—I have a couple but I'm not going to have some trigger-happy fool blowing things. Smith, you get me Thomason on the radio."

Later, DeWitt came over to where Fairlie sat with Raab and Winstedt. "You talked with Thrayn on the way here today," he said. "I want everything he said."

"I've already told you," Fairlie protested.

"You've summarized," said DeWitt. "That's not enough. I want every detail."

131

Fairlie felt tired, and he was cold, and the rations did not sit well in his stomach. But he tried to piece together the fragmentary facts that he had learned from Thrayn.

The Vanryn, he had learned, had come far down the scale since the days when they had conquered space. Now that long-past glory was a mere racial legend to them. Their forefathers, said the legend, had desired the stars in the sky. They had built cunning ships and machines, and they had flown to the distant stars, and landed upon strange worlds, some of them larger than Ryn. They had been lords of all the skies until, somewhere far out between the stars, they had met the Llorn.

The Llorn were dark and shadow-wrapped and powerful. They had fought the Vanryn star-lords and had beaten them, again and again. They had forced them back to Ryn, and on a day of terror never to be forgotten, they had smitten and destroyed the cunning ships of the Vanryn, and had warned the Vanryn never to leave their world again.

For a long time, the Vanryn had hated that restriction. But after a while, they had come to change their ideas. They saw that their attempts to conquer the stars, their clever ships and machines, had all been wicked folly. It was themselves that they must conquer. They must cease their obsessions with material things and cultivate the spirit. They must discover how to live happily and simply, and not concern themselves with foolish and crass scientific vanities.

"It's hard to believe any intelligent people would adopt such a viewpoint," said Winstedt.

Raab dissented. "It's not hard to believe at all. They were a proud people, they met the Llorn, they were defeated. So they did what most people do—they rationalized their defeat. They didn't want to conquer space after all, they said, they turned their back on it purposely."

Fairlie thought that Raab had the right of it. A whole triumphant race and culture had, after shattering defeat, turned its face around and denied all its former values. And with the passing of time, what was only rationalization at first had become

132

true, and what they had said they believed they did now believe.

"Except for Thrayn," put in DeWitt when he said that. "He, at least, still has a spark of the old Vanryn vision. He can help us, if the others won't."

"Help us do what?" Fairlie said. "I told you what he said, that there are no machines, no secrets, down in that city, that all that was long ago. And all the more ancient places like the Hall of Suns are just ruins and—" He stopped. The sudden stiffening of DeWitt told him of the blunder he had made, in mentioning the one name he hadn't meant to mention.

"The Hall of Suns?" said DeWitt softly. "What's that? You didn't mention that before, Fairlie."

"Some old ruins that Thrayn spoke of that he'd seen—that's all I know," said Fairlie.

"You're sure that's all you know?"

"Of course I'm sure."

"The Hall of Suns," DeWitt repeated, as though the name was music in his ears. "It's a fine name, isn't it? A fine ringing name, that sounds like the old Vanryn. We'll have to find out more about that. What exactly did he say?"

Fairlie tried to remember. "I have seen the Hall of Suns, I have dreamed of the ships of old—"

"Ah," said DeWitt. "I think we're on the right track after all. That down there"—he waved toward the valley—"may not be anything. But Thrayn is the key to something." He bent forward and his voice was suddenly fierce. "The next time we see him you tell him we want to know more about that Hall of Suns, Fairlie. Where it is, what it is. How to get there. And—no more little slips of memory."

Fairlie's bristles went up. "Or what? Maybe you'll threaten to kill me too, is that it? And then who'll talk to the Vanryn for you?"

DeWitt said grimly, "Maybe no interpreter would be better than one who's against me."

"Do we have to bicker between ourselves?" interrupted

133

Winstedt. "Haven't we got trouble enough? I mean, do we have any idea what the people down there are going to do?"

DeWitt laughed, and got to his feet. "Worried about your tender skin, Winstedt?"

"I'm not afraid," said Winstedt angrily. "I just wish I knew what was going to happen tomorrow."

Fairlie wished that, too. He lay in his damp, chill sleeping-bag and looked up at the lofty dark tree-branches and the yellow-glowing night sky, and could not sleep for a long time. When he did sleep, his dreams were bad. The Vanryn were pouring up the slope and attacking them with strange weapons, only in the dream they suddenly weren't Vanryn at all but the Llorn, silent shadows who were trying to get into his mind and mustn't be allowed to do that.

He awoke to find his face wet from a light drizzle. It was dawn, and the men, looking dirty and unshaven, were climbing out and stretching and yawning.

Fairlie looked down in the valley. The black buildings, the tree-sheltered city, was silent and without activity, in the mist and smother. He was on the world of a distant star and this was what it was like—dismal and gray and heavy.

The light rain stopped, but the clouds did not lift. And as the day wore on, the city below remained silent and lifeless.

"They're staying indoors," said DeWitt. "Talking, probably, about us. All right, let them talk. We can wait till they get used to the idea of us."

They waited. They sat around the tracs up here on the ridge, and did not go near the city, and none of the people of the city came near them. Once in a while they saw figures come out and peer in their direction, but none of them came up the slope.

All that day nothing happened, not a thing. It seemed incredible to Fairlie, a fantastic situation, this stand-off. The men of Earth on the ridge and the men of Ryn in their city, curiosity on one side and fear and hostility on the other, trying to wait each other out.

The hours went by, and the ocher-colored twilight came on,

and still not a thing had happened. DeWitt went to talk with Thomason by means of the radio in one of the tracs, and Muirhead came and stood beside Fairlie and looked down into the valley.

"We're not getting anywhere," said Muirhead. "Those people don't want us here. Do we just wait around till they work themselves up enough to come up and cut our throats?"

Fairlie shrugged, and nodded toward the trac. "Ask him."

"I'll ask him nothing," said Muirhead. "I think he's a little nuts."

DeWitt's voice called them together a few minutes later. His face a white blur in the gathering darkness, he spoke brusquely. "We keep watches again tonight. Hagulian and Fairlie take the first, then Smith and Muirhead, then Winstedt and Raab."

"What do we do tomorrow?" asked Winstedt.

"We wait," said DeWitt. "We came here for something, for information. We don't go till we get it."

There was a strained and unhappy silence but nobody said anything.

DeWitt turned away, then turned back and said, "Everything's okay at the ship, Thomason says, except one thing. Christensen died this afternoon." He turned and went on, toward the trac, and started hauling out his sleeping-bag.

There was a silence.

Fairlie took his position, at the edge of the camp where he could look down at the valley, and Hagulian went to the other side. He sat down, and looked at the few lights down there. There was no sound now except the sough of the damp wind and the rustle of dark branches high overhead against the faintly glowing cloud-cover.

He felt a deep sadness. He had known when they left the ship that Christensen could not live. But he had discovered long ago that knowing a thing like that in advance did not entirely soften the shock and pain of it when it actually happened.

He supposed that they would bury Christensen near the ship. Whether or not any of them ever got back to Earth, Christensen

135

would stay here. It seemed odd that he should have come so far to find a grave, so far not only in space but in time. Christensen had been fifty-five, that meant he had been born in 1910. His first boyhood memories, in the little Minnesota town where he grew up, must have been of the old World War One days. Country roads deep in mud, and Model T flivvers churning along them, and people talking about the Kaiser, and marvelling every time they saw an airplane.

How could the boy Christensen ever have dreamed that he would come so far as this? And oh God, Fairlie thought, how could any of us have dreamed in the old innocent years of the road that we were going down faster and faster? It's been thrown at us too fast, he thought, each time the break-through has been bigger, until the nerves of wonder and awe get numb. Atomic bombs, atomic power, satellites, manned satellites, moon-rockets, all coming so fast together you had no time to evaluate or adjust.

And then the biggest break-through of all, the one the world didn't even dream of yet, the cavern in Gassendi and the things that were in it. Not only the secrets of a lost science that had led them out on this shadowed journey to Altair, but the tremendous and shattering implications about man's own past that would come down like an avalanche on every human being on Earth, when they were revealed.

How much can we take, Fairlie wondered. Can't we ever pause in all this progress long enough to find out where we're going? Chris tried to win a pause, a breathing-space, but he failed, he's dead. And maybe it's useless to try, we set our feet on this road long ago and maybe we have to go down it to the end, no matter what that end may be?

Fairlie sat and thought of these things until suddenly they were swept clear from his mind and he sprang to his feet, and looked wildly off into the darkness. The heavy wind had brought a sound to his ears, rising and falling, faint and sweet, and it was a sound he knew very well, one that set his skin to prickling.

It was the sound of a woman's voice and it sang the wordless song he knew.

20

THREE HUNDRED centuries dropped away and the woman of the song lived again and her singing was intimately and personally for him.

Fairlie stood up listening, with an eerie thrill on him colder than the wind and his heart beating high and fast. The voice called to him out of the darkness and he saw her standing on some high place with the stars wheeling around her like bright birds and he knew that he could go to her and she would be warm flesh and not a memory and a dream.

The wind sighed over the dark valley. The camp slept. The song came faint and sweet and silver-clear from somewhere far down the slope, calling, calling, and now the gap was not three hundred centuries of time but only a few hundred yards of land, easily crossed.

Fairlie began to cross them.

The woman sang and a very great hunger possessed Fairlie, a longing that had been with him since first that little silver sphere gave up its music all that time ago on Earth when this had all started. The hunger and the longing had driven him on this insane voyage, had brought him here to this alien planet under a foreign sun, and now they were about to be satisfied.

His feet pressed quietly against the sodden leaves, making no sound. The clouded sky cast little light. He moved in the night, among the very dark shadows of the trees, between the black solid trunks and under the branches of them, and the song led him.

The song made flesh. And it was just the same as he had always heard it, every note, every—

No.

It was not the same.

The elation, the high eerie beautiful thrill, began to go out of him. He moved more slowly, listening, wondering, trying to understand why.

He knew every note, every inflection. They were not appreciably changed. This voice was clear and lovely, with the same pure sound. But it was not the same. He knew now.

It was the voice of Aral that was singing.

The woman of long ago had sung to the stars. Her song was not intimate, not personal. It was a hymn, a trumpet call, a cry of joy and triumph for a whole race, a salute to brave and gallant men who had conquered the farthest horizons.

Aral's song was only a song, as shallow and pretty as herself, a thing to use to get something she wanted.

The night was empty again and reality pressed chill and damp on Fairlie. But he kept on walking.

He found her in a dark glade where bank and tree gave shelter from any prying eyes. She sat singing on a boulder at the edge of a stream, trailing a long twig in the water. He spoke her name and she put a hand on his shoulder, pressing him down into the blackness beside the big rock. Her voice never faltered. He could see her above him in the gloom, idly trailing her twig and singing, and her eyes darting all the while to this part of the glade and that as though she could see like a cat in the dark, as perhaps she could.

Fairlie suddenly felt a small stir of alarm. This did not have the feeling of a tryst. He was not very familiar with trysts, but he thought they would not be like this. He began to peer around anxiously himself, not knowing what he was looking for and not being able to see anything anyway, and then her song trailed off casually as though she had simply tired of singing and she slid down very close to him. He had to move his arm to make room for her and quite without knowing how it happened he had it around her and she was pressed up against him, all curves and angles and suppressed vitality. Her hair smelled with a wild sweetness of piney-soap and wood-smoke.

"You must be careful," she said, whispering. "They are watching the slope. That's why I didn't dare come to you, for fear they would catch me and punish me as they have done to Thrayn."

Fairlie stiffened. "What have they done to Thrayn?"

"He is shut up in a place, not allowed to come out. They're very angry with him. And with me, but mostly with him." Fairlie knew she smiled. "That is the advantage I have, being a woman." She put her hand up to his face and drew their two heads together and he felt her lips brush his, very lightly, almost as though by accident.

"I'm afraid for Thrayn. I want you to help me get him away."

This was not, definitely not, a tryst.

He pushed her back from him a little. She was wrapped in a cloak and the cloak was damp. Her hair was damp and her hand and cheek were cold from the night air. The ground under him and the boulder behind his back had already chilled him pretty well to the bone. Even without the reminder about Thrayn he would not have been feeling very romantic.

"I wondered why he didn't come back," Fairlie said. "We've been waiting for him."

"Yes. And it's because of you that he's a prisoner. They're talking—oh, all sorts of things."

"What kind of things?"

"They seldom kill. I can't ever remember an execution. But this time I don't know. If anything should happen—"

"Like what?"

"Anything bad. Anything at all. They're afraid." She moved close to Fairlie again, clinging to him. "So am I. We've been safe and peaceful for so long and now everything's different and it's

139

exciting but I can't help being afraid. I thought I didn't believe in the Llorn. But now I'm not sure."

Mechanically Fairlie put both arms around Aral and held her close. "You really think they may kill him?"

"If he was free we could go to another community a long way off and everything would be all right. Please help me. Please. I'll give you—"

"Hush up," he said harshly, "and let me think."

He and the other Earthmen were certainly responsible for what had happened to Thrayn. He had not wanted to lead them here, and they had insisted. It might have been partly Thrayn's fault for being curious about the ship in the first place.

I feel doubly responsible, Fairlie thought, because I was the one who did the talking, no matter whose idea it was. And now I have opened my big stupid mouth about the Hall of Suns and DeWitt will never rest until he finds it. Which means that he has to have Thrayn, who has been there. Which means that if I know DeWitt there will be the devil to pay in that town if they don't give up Thrayn to him.

It wasn't good. Anyway you looked at it it was not good. But anything was better than having DeWitt deal with it. Fairlie's mind raced ahead, seeing DeWitt and his guns coming into the town, and some people dying, and the inevitable reprisals and more people dying. Perhaps in the end their whole party, even possibly the whole expedition. It would be much better if Thrayn simply escaped right now, quietly and without fuss.

And that meant that he, Fairlie, had to do it.

He shook his head and groaned.

Her chilly little hands were on his face again, her cold little muzzle shoved passionately against his neck. "Please? It isn't that I'm in love with Thrayn. You understand that?"

"I understand completely," Fairlie said. He told her briefly what he thought of her in English, which she did not understand, and hauled her roughly to her feet. "Let's go."

She stood still for a moment facing him and he thought she

140

was puzzled by his response which was not at all what she had expected.

"I thought you liked me," Aral said. "I sang to you because I thought you would hear my voice and come here and you did. But why did you come if you don't like me?"

He countered with another question. "Where did you learn that song?"

"From the old records," she said carelessly. "Everybody knows it. It was some kind of a hymn, in the old days. Every year they had a big gathering at the Hall of Suns and it was sung there."

"Have you been to the Hall of Suns?" asked Fairlie, momentarily tempted.

"No," Aral said. "Only Thrayn, I think, out of our whole community. Most of them don't care about such things."

"Well, let's get on with it," Fairlie said, feeling suddenly a little sick. And how things get mixed up, he thought. I have to play into DeWitt's hands by getting Thrayn away so he can lead DeWitt to the Hall of Suns which I don't want DeWitt to find, because I can't leave Thrayn possibly to die and DeWitt won't leave him where he can't act as guide.

Oh, hell.

And there is another thing, a very interesting speculation. It is this. What will Thrayn's people do to me if they catch me?

Aral was several steps ahead. She stopped and looked back at Fairlie. "Aren't you coming?" she asked. "What's the matter?"

"Never mind," he said. "Just go on."

She led him, careful and crafty as a nocturnal hunter moving on soft paws. The mist was thick in the folds of the slope. She clung to these places and then to the sheltered lower bottoms where the stuff was like layers of white cotton-wool rolling over and over wherever the wind could get at it.

Fairlie lost himself completely. He waded through cold water, trying not to slosh, and he squelched in mud and stumbled in tangled reeds, and then there was grass slippery with damp and then pavement of some iron and indestructible plastic that was

141

nevertheless worn into humps and hollows by the passage of countless centuries and innumerable feet. And now there were walls around the two of them, and windows, and occasional lights and sounds.

Aral became even more stealthy and cautious. She crept. She flitted. She saw and heard all ways at once. It dawned on Fairlie that this was a talent born of long practice. She loved it. He could see her as a small child roaming quick and furtive through these streets, full of a giggling mischief, peering at windows and peeping at keyholes, feeling the triumphant superiority of one who cleverly watches unseen while his stupid victims do all sorts of things never intended for the public eye.

A tricky little piece altogether, thought Fairlie. But she's good at it. She's awfully good. We might even make it if I can keep from falling over my own feet.

The town smelled of ancientness. It felt of ancientness when he touched it, of substance crumbling away molecule by molecule, atom by atom, under beating suns and washing rains, under heat and frost, under the rubbing, grinding pulverizing weight of years adding up in the thousands. Not old, as Thrayn had said, like the ruins. But old enough. Many of the buildings were empty and Aral kept to these deserted areas as much as she could.

But this aid quickly ran out on them and there were more and more lights in more and more windows and Aral began to dance on the tips of her toes, her face shining with the unholy excitement of the game. And it's well and good for her, thought Fairlie. If we're caught she can always say I forced her to lead me and they won't touch her, but me—

He thought he had been scared before, and he had been, but he was learning that there are many kinds of fear and that each one has its own unique charm. He thought when he got home he could write a book about the art of being scared.

A voice sounded in the street ahead of them. Aral peeped around a corner and then motioned him to come on. Fairlie followed with extreme caution. There was something odd about the

142

sound of the voice, something a little unnatural. Aral beckoned to him impatiently. He saw that the street was empty, dim with the pervading mist, gleaming dully where the window-light fell on the wet surfaces.

The voice came from inside one of the buildings. It was a very strong, very authoritative voice and it was not conversing, it was making a speech. Or perhaps it was a sermon. Fairlie could not distinguish any words at first but as he and Aral approached the building the acoustics improved and he began to pick up a phrase here and there. The man was talking about truth.

"It is not to be found," he said, "in those vast wastes beyond the sky. We explored them and what did we find? Nothing but evil and death. Now we know that we must look within ourselves for truth, the real meaning of existence."

The prancing assurance of Aral's gait suddenly lessened. Fairlie caught a look of doubt on her face. She glanced sidelong at him and then moved to a window of the building and looked in. Rashly, he thought, until he joined her and looked for himself.

"The soul," said the so-strong, so-sure voice. "That is the important thing. Not ships, not machines, not the cold glittering things that we had come to worship. No. Man's understanding of himself, his ability to enrich every moment of his life with quiet pleasure—this is our true goal. And we must—"

The floor of the building was very large and it was sunk below the level of the ground so that Fairlie seemed to be looking into a big and richly decorated cave. Sweeping ramps curved down into it. Slim columns of some reddish metal, severely plain but beautiful in their soaring cleanness of line, upheld the roof.

The plastic floor still held a dim geometrical pattern suggestive of unfettered space and the walls had some sort of mural decoration done apparently with metallic wires that gleamed in the lamplight but too faintly for their real form to be discerned. The lamps made a clustered blotch of light in the midst of this hugeness, and here the men were gathered, two or three hundred of them, listening in silence to the speaker.

143

And the speaker was a tiny silver sphere revolving in a plastic box.

"From the old records," Aral had said about the song. "Everybody knows it." Fairlie looked down at the crowd and the little silver ball and he understood something that had puzzled him ever since he first met Aral in the ruins.

That was why the language had not changed much. They still listened to the imperishable records, still learned from them, and so their speech pattern had remained almost constant all this time.

"This is our strength," said the voice of the sphere, speaking out of the bitter nightfall of the race. "This is our hope and our salvation. We have been like children, and we have seen the results of our childishness. In suffering our eyes have been opened and we have become men. Now we know the difference between truth and falsehood, between that which is worth having and that which is nothing. For the first time, then, we are free."

Aral plucked at his sleeve. "Let's hurry while they're all inside." She led him swiftly away, but now her face was shadowed and uneasy.

"Have you heard that speech before?" Fairlie asked her.

"I know it by heart. And I always used to sneer at it, but that was before your ship came. The Llorn were so long ago—" She added irritably, "Oh, come on, don't be so slow and clumsy."

Fairlie swallowed his annoyance and followed her. The words of the ancient speaker rang in his ears. *For the first time, then, we are free.* He walked in the hollow empty streets, between the dark buildings and the crumbling walls and the little weak glimmers of lamplight. He looked at Aral. And he wondered.

She brought him to a narrow passageway between two buildings and led him into it, signalling the greatest of caution. At the far end she halted, pressed back against the wall, and pointed with her chin.

Fairlie looked.

About twenty feet away there was a building no different from any of the other buildings except that a man sat in front of it. The door of the building was open and the windows were not barred. There was nothing to prevent anyone inside from coming out except that the man who sat in front of it held in his hands a sort of reaping-hook, a peaceful agricultural implement perfectly capable of slashing people as well as grain.

"Thrayn is in there," whispered Aral. "All you have to do to free him is to get Grahan out of the way." Quite unnecessarily she added, "Grahan is the man with the hook."

21

EASY, FAIRLIE THOUGHT. All I have to do is get Grahan out of the way. No trick at all.

He looked at Grahan, who sat facing the door and with his back to Fairlie. He seemed to be a man in the prime of muscular middle-age and the cloak-wrapped shape of him appeared as uncompromising as a block of stone. Thrayn, quite obviously, had not had any desire to come out and tackle him.

Fairlie did not have any either.

"Well?" whispered the girl impatiently.

Fairlie said, "I'm planning."

The open door and window were an illuminating sidelight on this peculiar culture. It meant that they had no regular facilities for restraint, in other words no jail, which meant that there was not enough crime to bother about.

The reaping-hook in the hands of the guard was another. He thought that DeWitt, with his ideas of great powerful weapons, should see that.

At that, Fairlie thought, the reaping-hook would be adequate enough if it was turned his way.

"What is it?" asked Aral scornfully. "Are you afraid?"

Fairlie gave her a cold look. "Find me something," he said, holding out his hand with the fingers crooked. "Something heavy, a stone, a chunk of cement."

He crouched down and carefully took off his shoes. The wind

came sucking and sighing down the passageway. Fairlie waited, shivering, looking at Grahan sitting twenty feet away from him. Grahan kept getting larger and the blade of the reaping-hook got longer. Stray gleams of light from the door and window glinted on the sharp edge of it, the thin curved point. Fairlie was fascinated by it. He could not take his eyes away from it. He started violently when Aral came back soft-footed as a shadow and put something cold and heavy into his hand.

He waited a minute longer but now there was nothing to wait for and so he moved forward out of the passageway into the open square, and it was like standing on the end of the high diving-board until you were ashamed to stand there any longer and you stepped off into nothing and it was a long long way down to the water but you couldn't change your mind.

His feet were freezing, wet socks cold against the chill wet pavement. He ran. He felt clumsy, his legs and arms were awkward sticks. He did not make any noise. The heavy thing Aral had given him weighed his hand down. He ran with a million dark windows peering down at him, he ran naked and obvious if anyone should look, and all at once Grahan was right in front of him. In a frenzy of haste he lifted the weighted hand and Grahan began to turn around. He must have heard something, a rustling or a hard-drawn breath behind him.

Fairlie knew it must all be happening in a split-second but it seemed to be drawn out very slow and deliberate, Grahan's head turning and showing part of a hard-featured face gone slack with surprise and alarm, the great curved blade lifting in the first segment of a sweeping arc that would end at Fairlie's throat. A raw wild panic leaped in Fairlie but it had the odd effect of steadying him. His eye was suddenly keen, his hand unerring. Grahan fell. The reaping-hook fell with him.

And it was easy.

Aral came running. She went inside the building. Fairlie put down the thing he had had in his hand and picked up the reaping-hook instead. Grahan lay still. As an afterthought Fairlie bent to see if he was breathing. He was.

Fairlie began to shake violently. How easy it is, he thought. I might just as well have killed him. I didn't consciously *not* kill him. So easy when he swung the hook at me.

Thrayn and Aral came out of the house. They ran back to the passageway and Fairlie ran with them. "Here," he said to Thrayn, "you take this." He handed him the hook. He scrabbled his shoes on again. "Let's go. Let's get the devil out of here."

He glanced back at the dark lump lying in front of the building. It dawned on him that he was making a lot out of nothing, simply because he had never done anything like that before. De-Witt had done precisely the same thing to him and never turned a hair.

It was easy.

"You could have done that yourself," he said to Aral. "Why did you need me?"

"I might have been caught," she said, and gave him a gamin smile.

"So might I. But better me than you, is that it?"

"We'll all be caught if we don't clear out of here," Thrayn said. He pushed Aral in front of him. They ran, and Thrayn carried the reaping-hook over his shoulder.

Again they clung to the most deserted streets, and again Fairlie lost all sense of direction. After a while he began to hear noises somewhere behind them, a large muttering punctuated by sharp cries. The three of them stopped to listen.

"They've found Grahan," Thrayn said. "The whole town will be after us now."

The muttering surged and grew, moving through unseen streets, clamoring against distant walls.

"We'll have to make a big circle around," said Aral.

"Well, make it, then. I don't want to have to use this." Thrayn shook the reaping-hook. In the chill gloom their faces were pale and scared. Up to a point Aral had been having fun. Now she was not having any fun.

She whined, "I'm tired."

The muttering swelled, roared, grew, menaced.

148

Fairlie smacked Aral hard across the buttocks. "You haven't got time to be tired." He said to Thrayn, "Get on. You'll be safe in camp."

His voice had a new note in it. They looked at him, startled, and ran on again. He loped behind them and for the first time in his life he felt as though he was the strong one, the man of action by whom the others would stand or fall.

With these two, he thought, it was not much of an achievement.

The noises behind them lessened. The edges of the town were passed. There was a very long period of stumbling and scrambling about in the wet and mire, the cold wind and the dark. Aral began to whine again and Fairlie handled her so roughly that she was glad to go back to depending on her own legs. Thrayn didn't whine, but he cursed a good bit and his cursing didn't strike Fairlie as much better. Thrayn was in a mess and he didn't like it. So far Fairlie had not heard one word of thanks from either of them for getting Thrayn free.

He was about out of patience when at long last they saw fires ahead of them and came into the camp, Fairlie shouting ahead good and loud so there wouldn't be any doubt about who it was.

DeWitt was waiting for him, looking angry. Behind him the camp was waking up and men were putting more wood on the fires and blinking nervously around.

"What the devil—" snarled DeWitt, and then he saw Thrayn and Aral and stopped. Aral collapsed like a rag doll onto somebody's blanket and Thrayn dropped beside her.

Fairlie sat down on a log and looked at DeWitt. "I have your Hall of Suns for you," he said, "and I'd advise you to start for it just as fast as you can." He nodded toward the valley and the town. "They don't like us. Not at all."

The man who had replaced Fairlie on lookout duty turned around from where he was standing at the edge of the camp and said, "There's an awful lot of lights down there, I can see 'em in the mist moving around."

"What did you do?" said DeWitt to Fairlie.

149

Fairlie told him, briefly, while Raab listened and weighed him coldly from behind DeWitt's shoulder. And DeWitt stared at Fairlie as though he didn't believe what he saw.

"I didn't think you had it in you. Oh, I know you didn't do it for me, you were thinking of *his* neck."

"And the trouble you'd make in that town."

"Sure, sure. But I still didn't think you had it in you." He grinned at Fairlie, a grin of honest approval, and turned away to give orders about breaking camp.

Fairlie got up and went over to Thrayn and picked up the reaping-hook that lay where Thrayn had dropped it.

"DeWitt," he said.

DeWitt looked at him.

"I have something for you. A sample of the mighty armaments of the Vanryn." Fairlie tossed the reaping-hook.

DeWitt caught it, looked at it, then looked again at Fairlie. "You have a funny sense of humor," he said, "but it doesn't amuse me."

Fairlie spoke to Thrayn. "He doesn't believe this is a weapon."

Thrayn lifted his head from where he had been resting it in Aral's lap. "It's true. We haven't any weapons. We haven't needed any since—" He broke off, his face sullen and disturbed.

Fairlie translated.

"Since what?"

"Since we stopped trying to fight the Llorn." Thrayn got up. He took Aral's hand and pulled her to her feet. "I don't think I want to go to the Hall of Suns. I don't want any more to do with this." He started off with Aral.

DeWitt stepped in front of him and pushed him back. "Wait a minute. What's he up to, Fairlie?" Fairlie told him. "Well, you tell him this. They were going to kill him, weren't they, and we got him out. He owes us something for that, doesn't he?"

When Fairlie had translated that, Thrayn glanced at DeWitt almost contemptuously and then looked at Fairlie. "*You* got me out, you and Aral together, and I expect you made your own bargain."

Fairlie was angry. And then he realized that Aral was not angry and that Thrayn had simply made a logical statement. Fairlie shook his head, baffled. "No bargain," he said. Then he asked Thrayn, "What are you afraid of?"

"Nothing. I just don't want to go, that's all."

"You're afraid, the whole town is afraid—afraid enough to kill you. Afraid enough to try and kill us if we don't leave them alone. Why? Do they think the Llorn are still watching them after all these thousands of years? Do they think just our presence here will bring the Llorn down on them again?"

Thrayn said, "Yes."

Fairlie looked at him and Aral. "And you believe this too?"

Aral said, "We don't know. But we don't want to find out."

"Why do you want to go there anyhow?" Thrayn demanded. "There's nothing but an old building."

The man who was on guard said worriedly, "Those lights down there—they seem to be coming this way."

DeWitt glanced at the tracs. The last piece of gear was being loaded in. The men were ready to move. He turned to Fairlie. "Tell these two people they have a free choice. They can lead me where I want to go, or they can wait right here, tied up hand and foot, for their own people to find them. Go on, tell them."

Fairlie told them.

Thrayn got a trapped and hunted look. Fairlie somehow could not muster as much sympathy for him as he should have. He said, "The Llorn are problematical but there's no doubt about your own people. Anyway, if there's nothing at the Hall of Suns, what harm can it do to lead us there?"

"All right," Thrayn muttered. "We'll go." He looked at DeWitt darkly. "But he may wish he hadn't."

They started for the tracs.

"What's he say?" DeWitt asked. "Nothing friendly, I could tell that."

Fairlie explained, and DeWitt laughed.

"The Llorn again? I wish they were still around. I'd like to meet a race that could put the fear of God into a people so that

151

all this time later it's still there. That's a real achievement."

DeWitt climbed into the trac and then, leaning down, he added, "By the way, tell your friends they can forget the idea they have in mind. They won't have any chance of escaping on the way." He raised his voice, shouting to the men. "Douse those fires! Come on!"

The glade went dark in a shower of kicked sparks. Motors coughed. Headlights glared out suddenly, bringing the tree-trunks into sharp relief. There was a brief confusion of men running, clambering aboard. Fairlie found his place in the trac next to Aral and Thrayn, with DeWitt on the other side of them. The trac heaved forward with a lurch and a roar. The others followed in a line behind it. DeWitt pulled out a gun and fired high into the air, the shots slamming flat and deadly over the noise of the tracs.

"That may hold 'em back a little." DeWitt leaned forward to Muirhead, the man at the wheel. "Take it fast. We want out of here."

Muirhead took it fast. The trac lunged and swayed. Great trunks slid toward them down the headlight beams, flashed past them at the last moment so close that the pattern of the bark was visible. Beside him Fairlie could feel Aral's body stiff with fear. He put his arm around her to steady her and she clung to him, hiding her face against his shoulder.

Thrayn hung onto the seat in a kind of daze. Fairlie was scared himself. He leaned his head back so that he could not see the tree-trunks leaping at him and saw instead a racing pattern of branches against a black sky, and suddenly the blackness appeared as a vast and bottomless gulf in which moved shadow-wrapped unhuman forms, and he shivered in a draft of interstellar cold, remembering nightmare.

22

IT HAD RAINED for four days. It had rained forever.

Fairlie wondered dully if he would ever be dry and warm and unmuddy again. For almost every hour of these days in which they had pressed northwestward under Thrayn's sullen guidance, the sodden downpour had fallen out of the heavy ocher sky. The going, in the forested valleys and up on the naked ridges, had got steadily worse. He thought that if it got much worse they would not go at all.

Trac Two was stuck again. That made the third time today, Rogers, its driver, not being as expert a driver as Muirhead. The heavy machine wallowed and roared like a mired dinosaur in the sticky brown clay of the slope, churning it to mud. Smith and Hagulian shoved, and at the wheel of Trac One, Muirhead pulled on the towrope. DeWitt gave angry orders. The rest of them stood in the rain and waited.

"I never thought," said Raab in a kind of grunt as he swabbed at his eyeglasses, "that a trip to the stars could be ruined by bad weather."

It did sound ridiculous when you put it that way, thought Fairlie. What kind of a trip did you have to Altair? Oh, terrible, it rained nearly the whole time we were there.

He looked at Aral. She sat on a stone with her cloak huddled around her and her cloak was dripping and her hair dripped, and she looked a little bit like a drowned cat. She stared at them with sulky hatred and said nothing.

At least, Fairlie thought, she had a cloak. Thrayn had not. Somebody had given him a windbreaker and worn over his tunic it looked quite incongruous. He stood near DeWitt—he had been warned at the start about getting too far away—and looked fixedly back at the rain-smothered landscape of hills, hogbacks and tree-choked valleys through which they had come.

Fairlie walked over to him, his shoes noisily slapping the water and mud. He said, in the Vanryn, "There hasn't been a sign of them so far."

Thrayn shrugged and made no answer.

"They wanted rid of us, didn't they? All right, we left the city, we're a long way from it. Why would they follow us?"

Thrayn gave him a gloomy look. "They would follow a little way, for certain. And when they saw where we were heading—"

"You mean, toward the Hall of Suns? Do they too know where it is?"

"Everyone on Ryn knows where it is," said Thrayn. "Even though nobody goes near it."

"But you went near it."

"Yes. Because I was a fool. And now I am paying for my folly, and I shall pay more, when they overtake us."

Fairlie said, "I just doubt they'd follow at all. No matter if they do dislike us—"

Thrayn gave him a bitter look and said, "Dislike? It is not the word. They fear you with a terrible fear because you bring a danger to Ryn that has not been for ages. You broke the commandment of the Llorn by coming here in a ship, and now you go to the Hall of Suns, the very shrine and center of the old Vanryn star-lust. Oh, yes, they will come after us and will try to kill you before you bring the Llorn upon us."

DeWitt turned brusquely, as with a bellow like a frantic elephant Trac Two lunged convulsively free of the mire. "What's all this he's getting off?" he demanded.

Fairlie told him, and DeWitt looked disgusted. "I thought he

154

had some guts, but I guess I was wrong. All that blabber of his people about the Llorn has finally scared him too."

Thrayn had turned his back on them and gone over to Aral. She was talking to him, with suppressed passion in the posture of her dripping figure, and Thrayn was listening somberly.

"Suppose he's right—suppose the Vanryn do come after us?" said Fairlie.

DeWitt stared at him. "If they do, we'll slap them back, that's all. I've been fighting people for nearly a year now, for this thing. I've fought bureaucrats, defense secretaries, Christensen, everybody, to get here. You can be damned sure those superstitious fools aren't going to stop me now."

He turned and bellowed through the rain. "Start walking! The tracs will have a hard enough time making this slope without carrying us."

Without enthusiasm, they started up the slope. They avoided the soft gashed track made by the two vehicles that were still laboring on up toward the ridge. But even so, the grass was slippery with water and it was an awkward climb. Raab, the oldest of them, proved surprisingly agile but Winstedt was puffing and groaning audibly by the time they reached the crest.

Fairlie, panting, looking away northwestward from their new vantage but there was nothing to be seen but more hills and valleys and hogbacks, shading rapidly into obscurity in the twilight and mist and rain.

"Which way from here?" DeWitt asked, and Fairlie put the question to Thrayn. Thrayn silently pointed.

"Ask him how far."

Thrayn shrugged. "Perhaps one day. Perhaps two."

DeWitt nodded toward a grove of trees farther along the ridge. "We'll camp there. Soon be dark, anyway."

It was a cheerless camp. They unloaded by the light of the electric lanterns, with the rain dripping remorselessly on them, while Hagulian and Muirhead tried to scrabble together enough dry wood to start a fire. Muirhead had lost his knife and argued

155

angrily when Hagulian wouldn't lend his. Their tempers were all strained too hard, Fairlie thought.

A little later, he looked at the others as they crouched around the fire. Winstedt had got a piece of tarpaulin and had it over his head so that he looked ridiculously like an old woman in a shawl. Raab pulled his lip in thought and looked at the flames, and DeWitt was trying to keep his photo-maps dry as he studied them, his hard, flat brown face poked almost into the lantern. Beyond him Aral whispered to Thrayn, and across the fire the other men were dark lumps who said little but had weariness and discontent in every line of them.

The conquerors of space, Fairlie thought sourly. That's what we are. Only we don't look like it. We look like what we really are—a bunch of city-bred men camping in wet woods and not liking it, and it makes not a bit of difference that the woods are a long, long way from Earth.

DeWitt folded up the map. He said, "We should hit high country tomorrow. That checks with what Thrayn said, doesn't it?"

Fairlie nodded. "He said the Hall of Suns was up high."

"Good," said DeWitt. "By tomorrow night, we'll have it." In the firelight, his eyes were bright with secret triumph.

Raab looked at him, and said, "Have what? Do you really think you're going to find anything big after all this time?"

DeWitt smiled. He was near to his goal, and feeling very sure now. "We found things at Gassendi after all that time. We found plenty."

"You know yourself that was a different matter," said Raab. "The Moon is a natural deep-freeze to preserve anything. But how long would such things last in this?" He swept his hand to indicate the rain hissing down into the fire.

DeWitt, unperturbed, got to his feet. "We'll see," he said calmly, and went away.

"Christensen was right," Raab said. "He's a perfect example of the single-minded man. He believes he'll find things, because he wants to find them, no matter what reason says."

156

"I don't know," said Fairlie.

"You don't know what?" asked Raab irritably.

"Does it ever occur to you that DeWitt has carried it off all the way on this thing, right from the first, despite all that reason said? He forced those generator-tests at any risk, and they worked. He insisted a ship could be built, and lied and schemed until it was built. And now we're here, he's found a clue to something. Suppose we're all wrong again, and he gets hold of something big at the Hall of Suns?"

Raab stared at him, and said, "That's an uncomfortable thought. I've felt sure this trip was useless, that he couldn't find anything."

"But if he does?"

"If he finds powers or weapons beyond anything we know," Raab said slowly, "there's no doubt what he'll do. He'll take them triumphantly back to Earth for our people, and the first time the people on the other side of the Curtain hear about them, we'll have an explosion."

"Do we try to prevent that, if it looks like happening?" asked Fairlie.

In his mind he heard again Christensen's weak voice. "Try to hold him down."

Raab said unhappily, "I guess we'd have to try." He did not seem to want to talk about that possibility. He went and got his sleeping-bag and spread it out beside a tree-trunk and got into it. Most of the others were making their beds in or under the tracs.

Fairlie remained, staring at the dying fire and thinking. Try to hold him down. And how would you hold down a man like DeWitt when he grabbed for the greatest power in the stars, if he actually got it into his hand?

He looked at Thrayn and Aral. They lay beside each other near the other side of the fire, motionless as though asleep. But a sound came murmuringly from them, and he knew it was Aral's voice whispering, whispering, to Thrayn.

"Aren't you going to get some sleep?" asked Winstedt. He still

157

sat with his tarp over him. He and Smith shared the first watch, but while Smith had taken up his post out in the shadows, Winstedt clung to the fire.

"In a minute," Fairlie answered, looking at Thrayn and Aral.

"You've got the next watch," Winstedt said querulously. "You needn't think I won't wake you for it. I need sleep too, this has been hard."

"Oh, all right," said Fairlie, and got his sleeping-bag and flung it down in the wet grass not far from Raab.

Water dripped on his face, and he swore softly. Then he remembered something that made him smile wryly. It was years ago when he had told his mother he was going to take up linguistics as his career. Relieved and happy, she had said, "I'm so glad you're going to follow something studious and safe, and not something dangerous."

Next morning, they woke to a welcome surprise. It was not raining. The sky was still somber with dark-yellow clouds, but it was an enormous relief not to have water trickling down your face, and spirits lifted.

"Just like home," said Muirhead. "Takes three–four days to work up a rain, then three–four days of rain, and then—" He stopped. The drizzle had begun again before he could finish the sentence.

"Then what?" asked Hagulian. And he added disgustedly, "You and your weather predictions."

DeWitt had started toward the trac in which the radio was, but now he turned around and came back. "I was going to have Thomason send one of the 'copters out to try and locate the place for us," he said. "But they couldn't see anything in this. Well, let's move."

For a moment, nobody moved. They just looked at DeWitt and then at each other. It wasn't rebellion, Fairlie thought, not even the spark of one. It was only that they were sick of the hard going, and wanted DeWitt to know it.

"If anybody doesn't want to come along," said DeWitt quietly, "he can stay behind."

158

There was no further hanging back. The tracs rolled, and the rain came down, and they could go on this way clear around Ryn, thought Fairlie.

DeWitt kept Thrayn beside him, and frequently questioned him through Fairlie, and then checked his photo-maps. Which of these forking valleys? Which way over the ridge ahead? In most cases, Thrayn answered with sullen briefness. He didn't know. He couldn't remember. He thought that this was the way but wasn't sure.

They had been gaining elevation all these days but now they began to climb in earnest. Some of the slopes were so steep that again they had to get out and walk. Winstedt complained loudly of his feet.

On one of these occasions, Fairlie took the opportunity to walk beside Aral. She had changed a good bit. That first night in the ruins she had been mocking and beautiful, and that other night by the city she had been a cunning, calculating sex-box, but she was none of these things now. She was small and wet, and fear and anger and tiredness had made her face tight and mean.

"You talk a good bit to Thrayn," said Fairlie.

Aral flashed him a hostile look. "And why not?"

"It depends on what you're telling him," said Fairlie. "I've a strong idea you're urging him into trying to run off."

"And if I am?" she said viciously. "Do we owe you our lives? You are madmen who will bring on destruction, either from the Llorn or from my people to prevent the coming of the Llorn. Must we be destroyed too?"

"You said the Llorn were only a legend, not long ago," he reminded.

"Thrayn said that, not I," Aral answered. "He was wrong, just as he was wrong to let his curiosity make him go to see your ship. And my people are right, when they say that you and your ship and your pryings will bring the shadowed ones again to Ryn."

Her raw fear was perfectly sincere, Fairlie thought. He was

159

not surprised, when he thought about it. It was one thing to be skeptical about the existence of the Llorn, as Thrayn and she too to some extent had been, when nobody had thought much about the Llorn for ages. But one or two people could not hold out psychologically against a great number, and the ancient dread that had now re-awakened in the Vanryn had infected Aral too. It was a natural consequence that she should infect Thrayn with it.

"Don't talk to him so much," said Fairlie, curtly, and went on ahead.

That was the last slope they had to negotiate on foot for now they had come up out of the maze of valleys and ridges onto a high, rising plateau. The gray wall of rain prevented them from seeing more than a few hundred yards ahead, and clumps of trees loomed up spectrally through the mist and dropped behind them into obscurity again.

By late that afternoon the rain had got harder and there was wind behind it, blowing it right into their faces. Finally, unable to see far enough ahead to drive, Muirhead and Rogers stopped the tracs in the lee of a thin grove.

The wind-driven rain hit them like a shower of icy needles. There was no keeping it out, and they turned their faces away from it and huddled, more wet and miserable than at any time so far. The rain lessened, even seemed to stop, but the wind strengthened and seemed to freeze their drenched clothing.

"We can't go on like this," said Winstedt. His plump face quivered as though he was about to cry. "I tell you, we can't, DeWitt."

"Oh, stop it," DeWitt said harshly. "You get a little wet and you want to give up. We're going right ahead."

Again, there was a silence, nobody saying anything, and DeWitt read that silence correctly. His face got stony and dangerous.

Thrayn uttered a cry. He had turned, was facing ahead. They all turned, and wonder of wonders, the sky ahead of them now was lighter than it had been for days—still clouded, but the

160

clouds less dark and heavy, and the freezing wind driving them fast across the heavens.

They could see, now. From the vast sweep of this high plateau rose a lonely mountain of medium size, a dark, stark mountain that looked a little odd in outline. It was at that mountain that Thrayn was staring, his face dark with strain and doubt, and Fairlie suddenly realized that they had come to the Hall of Suns.

23

PARTLY BECAUSE they were awestruck at the sight of their goal, and partly because they were too tired to move, the men simply stood where they were and stared for the space of several minutes. And while they watched the weather continued to change with the abruptness of weather in high places. The icy gale that had sprung up began to make clear places in the sky for the sun to shine through, so that long slanting fingers of smoky light stroked and shifted over the mountains. One of them touched squarely on the Hall of Suns and woke a brilliant flash of pure gold from its highest pinnacle, and then moved on. But it was light enough now for the men to see clearly.

The top of the mountain had been levelled to make a massive pedestal, and after all these thousands of years the pedestal still held its burden proudly and with indomitable strength. The mountain had not changed much. But the building that crowned it had suffered. Even at this distance and in that late and eerie light it was apparent that the massive domes of the Hall were shattered and its walls breached by the relentless weight of time. And still it was grand and beautiful, with the mighty approaches to it climbing in sweeping curves up the flanks of the mountain as though they were designed for whole populations to march upon abreast.

Fairlie looked at it, forgetting for the moment his chill discomfort and aware of a sudden stinging in his eyes, a mingling

162

of pride and grief. It was as though this ruined monument to a long-lost glory belonged personally to him. And that's foolishness, he thought, and then he thought, But it does belong to me, and to Smith and Muirhead, to Raab and Winstedt, even God help us to DeWitt, for the Vanryn built it and we are their children as surely as Thrayn and Aral.

The name rang in his head like a golden bell. The Hall of Suns.

DeWitt was shaking him rudely by the arm. DeWitt had no time for poetic thoughts or unproductive emotions. He had Thrayn in his other hand.

"Ask him," DeWitt said. "Are those approaches still intact? Can we get the tracs up there? Is the building reasonably sound or must we be careful of collapse?"

Fairlie asked the questions.

Thrayn shook his head. "I don't know. I can't tell you."

"He's lying," DeWitt said impatiently when Fairlie translated. He caught Thrayn by the front of his incongruous borrowed windbreaker and shook him. He said to Thrayn in English, "It won't do you one bit of good——"

"Tell him," said Thrayn to Fairlie, "that I never went any farther than this." His teeth rattled and he looked at DeWitt with vicious dislike.

Fairlie said sharply, "Let him go. He's never been in the place. He came this far and looked at it, but obviously he didn't have nerve enough to go on and actually climb the mountain."

DeWitt said, "Ask him why."

Fairlie asked.

Thrayn said, "Because that is where the Llorn came. It was pleasant and exciting to stand here and see the Hall of Suns and dream of past glories, but that was enough for me. I had no wish to go closer."

DeWitt smiled briefly. "Tell him he's going now."

But Thrayn had turned away and was standing with Aral, who kept her head averted from the distant Hall of Suns as though

163

even the act of seeing it was enough to invite destruction. Thrayn looked at Fairlie over her head.

"We've led you as far as we can. Now let us go."

Fairlie passed this on to DeWitt and added, "It's true, DeWitt. I don't see what more you can get out of them."

"Maybe nothing," said DeWitt, "or maybe everything. They know a lot about what went on here in the old days, from the legends and traditions. They can still help. Tell 'em they can come free or they can come captive, but they're coming. Get 'em in the trac." He began to call out to the men, his voice strident and excited. He seemed in a kind of wild good humor, looking at the ruined pile atop the mountain and smiling, clapping people on the shoulder, urging them into the tracs and on.

The men made no protest now. They were fired up at the sight of their goal. Probably none of them could have turned back now without a closer look. But Thrayn and Aral protested wildly. Fairlie felt a twinge of pity for them, the fear was so stark white in their faces, but there was nothing he could do. Aral made one convulsive movement as though she was about to do something violent, but Thrayn caught her arm and said something brief that Fairlie could not hear, and after that they allowed themselves to be herded into the trac.

The vehicles roared and churned toward the foot of the mountain, shattering the ancient quiet with man-made thunder. The wind blew like knives against them, stabbing their cheeks with cold, piercing their garments. The sky cleared, and the peak stood up black and somber against the copper sky.

Here and there the plateau was dotted with clumps of wind-twisted, stunted trees. The tracs kept clear of these, lurching and growling and floundering on. Then, approaching the base of the mountain, they passed the last trees and came to a flatter area, a wide expanse of broken paving that encircled the whole base of the peak.

"A land-area for flying craft," said Winstedt.

DeWitt nodded. "It must have been something when the Van-

164

ryn came flocking to this place, hey? Wouldn't that have been something?"

DeWitt stared upward, his eyes brilliant, and Fairlie followed his gaze. Stark and mighty up there on the flattened peak towered the building, so dark, so massive, that it seemed like a continuation of the mountain itself. It seemed to be oval in cross-section. Its sides leaned gently inward as they soared, toward a roof of domes that stepped up to a central dome that bulked black against the fading sky.

It was not graceful architecture, Fairlie thought. It was not even, in the strict sense, beautiful. The Vanryn had been looking for something far beyond mere beauty when they built here. The great dark structure, arrogant upon its mountain, was like a gigantic fist grabbing for the sky. It was the ultimate, frozen-forever expression of the Vanryn pride and glory. It was not beautiful, but it was overpowering.

The fading light showed the massive curving roadways that swept up around the mountain. And it showed them worn and cracked and blocked with rock-slides and debris. No vehicle could make it up there now.

"Here's where we walk some more," said Winstedt in a dismal voice, as the tracs stopped.

DeWitt was already out of the trac. His voice rang. "Make up packs. Bring the radio, the few guns we have, as many rations as possible. And hurry, before it gets dark."

The men hurried, working silently but fast. The same fever that powerfully gripped DeWitt had touched them, and Fairlie felt it also. Then he looked at Thrayn and Aral.

Aral's face was white with desperate terror as she looked up the side of the vast bulk. She said rapidly, "I will not go up there."

"You have to," said Fairlie. "He won't let you stay, he won't let anything delay him now. You'll be dragged, if necessary. Tell her, Thrayn."

Thrayn had fear in his own eyes but he looked at DeWitt's striding figure, then whispered urgently to Aral. Fairlie could guess what he was saying. We have to go but we'll get away as

165

soon as we can, we'll slip away somehow. Please trust me, Aral. Please.

Fairlie felt sorry for them and impatient with them and a little guilty about them, all at once. Yet he had told them the truth. Nothing was going to hold up DeWitt. Not now.

Strung out in a line, with DeWitt leading and Fairlie with Thrayn and Aral not far behind him, the men began to climb.

They went up the curving roadway in the glow of the dying light, in the cold wind. Fairlie was aware of the silence, the peculiar ringing silence of mountains where nothing speaks but the voices of rock and wind and sky. Thrayn moved slowly, his head bent, his feet dragging. Aral clung to him inside the circle of his arm. The way was difficult. In several places it was dangerous, where it was necessary to skirt the outer edge of a rock-slide, or climb over it.

They came around a curve of the circling roadway, and De-Witt paused and they paused with him. On either side of the road there rose a white statue of more than life size. Each was the statue of a man in oddly close-fitting garments, but they were not of the same man. That on the right was of a stocky, bullet-headed man with strength in every harsh line of his face. That on the left, which had lost an arm at the shoulder, was of a younger man, with the fine face of a dreamer. At the base of each statue was a brief inscription.

"Rondix of Amaran," Fairlie translated, reading aloud the inscription beneath the dreamer. And the other—"Haz of the Farther Cluster."

"And who were they?" said Winstedt, wondering. And then he pointed ahead. "Look, there are others farther along."

"I would say," Fairlie hazarded, "that they were heroes of the Vanryn star-conquests. If that's so——"

DeWitt interrupted. "Of course it's so. Look at those faces. They were no ordinary men. The star-captains of the old Vanryn, eh? By God, I'd like to have met them."

A chill feeling came over Fairlie. There was something in

166

DeWitt's hard, transfigured face that was very like the faces of the statues. Too like, he thought.

They went on. They passed between other statues, at regular intervals, but DeWitt would not pause again and the names were hard to read in the dying light.

Some of the statues had completely fallen. Others were still upright but had lost limbs. But whole or broken, they were equally impressive. In the gathering twilight the strong faces looked down at them, the faces of the men who had dreamed very far and had made their dreams come true, the faces of men who had sown the Vanryn seed far across the universe, as far even as Earth.

Is your face among them, Kalber? Do you have at least that much reward for the struggle and the dying?

It was almost wholly dark by the time they went between the last two statues and stepped onto the level surface of the mountain-pedestal.

Level, but not smooth. The Vanryn had smoothed the rock once but ages had eroded and pitted it. There was a halt while the electric lanterns were brought out. Holding one, DeWitt led the way across the flat stone expanse toward the vast, looming wall of the building.

In the wall, where they reached it, there were no doors or windows. There were not even the cracks between blocks that Fairlie had expected. The wall was seamless, dark and solid as the stone on which they stood. Its black overhang seemed to go up forever into the sky.

"This way," said DeWitt. "There'll be a way in somewhere."

He went forward with the lantern, moving now so fast that it was almost a trot, as intent as a questing hound. They had gone perhaps a hundred yards along the base of the wall when Smith, behind Fairlie in the column, stopped and uttered a sharp exclamation.

"What is it?" asked DeWitt, coming back at once. "What did you find?"

"Look," said Smith. "Look there, at the base of the wall."

He held the lantern so that its light illuminated the place at their feet where the solid wall met the flat stone on which they walked. They stared.

Fairlie could not see anything. Not a thing. Just the slightly roughened wall and the rough stone from which it rose. Not a— Then he saw. Smith had got down on his knees and had brushed away the dust and grit in the angle of the wall and floor. And between stone wall and stone floor, there was no joint of any kind.

"It's monolithic," said Smith, in a faltering voice. "One piece. The whole thing."

Fairlie felt a frozen incredulity. Oh, no, he thought, not even the old Vanryn could have done that. He looked again.

They had. They had not merely smoothed off the top of a stone mountain to make a pedestal for their Hall of Suns. They had built the Hall out of the mountain itself, carving the stone with unimaginable forces and cunning, shaping the whole top of the mountain into a gigantic monolith that was a building.

"What the hell difference does it make how they built the place?" said DeWitt, his voice raw with impatience. "It's what's inside we want to see. Come on!"

They went on, around the curve of the titan monolith, with the icy wind screaming and whooping at them and their little lantern-beam bobbing and quivering in the vast darkness. Then something flashed back the light from ahead.

There was a massive door, the two valves plated with bright gold, untouched and untarnished except that the doors themselves sagged drunkenly, one inward, one outward. They made Fairlie think of the broken, gigantic doors of Gassendi cavern as he had seen them in the picture. And how long ago that seemed now, and how far he had come since then.

DeWitt went between those sagging doors, and they followed. They stepped carefully over the scattered debris that had fallen from above. And ahead of them DeWitt's lantern angled down a long corridor of solid stone—a passageway through the mono-

168

lithic wall. The lantern bobbed up and down, for DeWitt was running now.

The lantern stopped. They came up to it and then, one by one, they stopped too. Fairlie saw DeWitt's face frozen and wild, and then, looking beyond him, he forgot about DeWitt.

Black space, endless space, the dark nothingness that is the very warp and woof of the cosmos, and somehow we have stepped into it, and stand in it, and all about us burn the great suns. Blue and yellow, green and red and violet-white, they blaze all around us, and we are naked and lost among them, we little men without even the shell of a ship around us. We stand in the cold dark without knowing how we came here, and the mighty stars burn pitilessly and their gleaming planets shine by their light, and how can this thing be?

Fairlie was forever grateful that as he stood there, his mind staggered and crushed and foundering in unreality, the prosaic voice of Smith sounded close in his ears.

"Good God, look at it! What an effect!"

An effect. Yes, thought Fairlie desperately, it is an effect, an illusion, we have not really fallen through into the emptiness between the stars. This is a building, and we are inside it. Repeat it, cling to it. This is an effect.

"For a minute," said Winstedt in an unsteady voice. "For a minute I thought—"

And voices were good. Men's voices were good, they brought you back, they got your feet on reality again, you could begin to understand.

We are not in infinite space. We are inside a hall whose huge-some vastness and darkness give that impression. These are not suns around us. They are glowing spheres, each with little planets cunningly fixed to it, each mounted upon a pedestal so thin and transparent as to be almost invisible. This is a model, a little artificial universe.

And it was a shattered universe, Fairlie saw now. Fragments of eroded stone had fallen, and pedestals had been smashed, and

169

the glowing suns they had borne had fallen and rolled to rest in the debris upon the floor. Fallen stars, still glowing.

Raab bent to examine one, his face eerily blue in the light of the azure globe. "Cold light," he said. "Perpetual, nearly. Not radioactive as we know it but on the same principle."

Nobody paid him any attention. They stood and looked, and now Fairlie saw that the highest dome, the lofty central peak, was open to the faintly-glowing clouded sky.

There was a small balcony in that opening. A winding stair led to it, around and around the looming, curving walls, and part of that stair had fallen.

It was up there, Fairlie thought, with sudden knowledge. Up there is where the woman sang.

DeWitt's strong voice, almost trembling with eagerness, brought them up short. "Let's have a look. We've got four lanterns—split into four groups. You come with me, Fairlie."

"This building could be dangerous—" Winstedt began.

DeWitt laughed with strange hilarity. "Dangerous, eh? But it was dangerous to come here, Winstedt. It was dangerous to build a ship and launch it but we did it, we made it here, and now you blabber about danger."

He grabbed hold of Fairlie's arm, and his hand quivered a little. "This way, Fairlie. There's an inscription on that pedestal. Read it. You back there—you watch Thrayn and the woman. Go ahead, Fairlie!"

It was the pedestal that upheld a blue-white sun-globe, and the light fell harsh on DeWitt's wild and eager face as Fairlie translated aloud the golden words about the pedestal.

"Bronic of Linar landed first upon the second planet of the star Quroon." He added, "There's a date too, but I don't yet know all their chronology."

"No matter," said DeWitt, holding him and pulling him on. "These are just commemorative inscriptions, that's clear. Let 'em go. There's more here than that."

And he went on, dragging Fairlie as though Fairlie was unwilling, and over their heads upon their tall pedestals shone the glowing suns and the gold words beneath proclaimed the discoverers, the first ones.

"Fennelin of the Dark World landed first upon—"

"Theramos of Korsh—"

Names. Names of glory, the pantheon of the Vanryn heroes. The very mighty men whose trophies had been suns.

But there was nothing more.

They came to the farther wall. The other lanterns bobbed toward them and the four groups met again, and among one group Fairlie saw the sick, scared faces of Thrayn and Aral.

"What?" asked DeWitt. "What did you find?"

There was a moment's silence. Then, in his cold precise voice, Raab said, "To me this has all the appearance of a great national monument, no more and no less. I do not think there were ever any laboratories or arsenals or secrets here."

The word was spoken, the thing they had all been thinking, and Fairlie almost did not want to see DeWitt's face in this moment of disastrous defeat.

But DeWitt spoke with harsh, undaunted determination. "You'd like to believe that, wouldn't you? But it isn't so. They didn't build this whole place just as a monument. You can't make me believe that."

"Can't I?" Raab said mercilessly, and for just a moment Fairlie saw, for the first time, the haggard shadow of defeat in DeWitt's eyes.

For a moment only. DeWitt's face hardened, and the old look came into it. Rip it out, make it go, force it the way you want it to go.

"Listen, Raab," he said. "The rest of you, too. There's something here. If not the secrets of the Vanryn, there'll be clues to where those secrets are. We're going to find them. We stay here till we do find them. Is that clear?"

"And if there's nothing to find?"

"We keep looking," DeWitt said. "We just keep looking."

Standing there in the cold, with the glow of the mock-suns

171

falling upon his face, DeWitt looked as uncompromising as the mountain.

With a flash of fatal foreknowledge, Fairlie knew that if De-Witt refused ever to admit defeat, none of them would return to Earth.

24

It was on the second night after this that those who followed them came to the Hall of Suns.

Fairlie was very tired. For most of the forty-eight hours that had passed, he had worked. They had all worked, and all their work so far had been for nothing. DeWitt had driven them, setting up search programs. There must be vaults beneath the great monolith. Find them. There could be hidden chambers within the solid-seeming walls. Dig them out. The great, faded golden inscriptions on the walls may contain clues of the utmost value. Translate them, Fairlie. All of them.

They had found no vaults. They had found no hidden chambers. And in the long inscriptions, Fairlie had found no clues, no secrets. In letters of imperishable gold the Vanryn had celebrated their conquest of many stars, and the names of the conquerors and the details of their splendid deeds were there, but no details of weapons, of scientific processes, or of the location of such things.

"Doesn't it seem logical to you," Raab had protested, "that the ships, the weapons, all those things, were just what was destroyed by the Llorn in that judgment day that annihilated the big starport?"

"Logic," DeWitt had said, and he had laughed. "Christensen was very logical about why we couldn't go to the stars, wasn't he? So was Rendell, so was everyone. And yet we're here. And here we stay till we get what we came for."

The men had sounded, dug, searched. Fairlie had transliterated and transcribed. He had translated when DeWitt bullied and threatened the scared Thrayn and Aral. And it was all for nothing and he was sick of it. They were all sick of it.

He was tired, and he was very cold. At sunset the sky had been finally swept clear of clouds by a hard north wind that had a wintry edge. The wind blew through every rent in the domes of the Hall, and except for those on watch the men had huddled around their lanterns in a corner a little protected from it. They had eaten in silence, looking almost as sullen if not as scared as Thrayn and Aral, and DeWitt had looked at them as though he realized their growing rebellious mood and was contemptuous of it.

Fairlie went outside, and shivered in the icy blast. Hagulian, one of the two men on watch on the great stone ledge outside the Hall, was blowing on his hands and muttering. Fairlie looked up and, for the first time in many nights, saw the heavens ablaze with unfamiliar stars.

He went back inside, but not to rejoin the others. He skirted the corner where they huddled, and took his way through the wrecked universe of glowing mock-suns to the main nave. The shining spheres, proud on their pedestals or lying fallen on the floor gave him light enough to see. He thought it a strange irony that the great trophies of the Vanryn star-conquerors should have come to this, that they served only to light the way for an insignificant stranger from afar.

Fairlie reached the base of the stair that wound up around the curving walls. He started up the stair. He looked up. Through the round opening high in the highest dome, the stars, the real stars, looked down at the mock-stars below.

"This is foolishness," he thought. "I'm taking unnecessary risks for nothing."

But he went on.

Higher and higher, and now the illusory suns below seemed

174

scarcely bigger and brighter than the real stars overhead. The wind whooped through the great opening above and made him shiver.

Now he must go carefully. The stair was broken not far above him, where it had joined onto the little balcony that projected out into the opening in the dome. It had been tested for strength, in these two days, and was safe up as far as the break, but he must be careful.

Fairlie stopped, a few yards down from where the stair ended in nothing. He sat down. He looked up at the small balcony, dark against the starry heavens.

That was the place, that balcony. There the woman of the Vanryn, three hundred centuries ago, had sung her splendid hymn to the stars and man. Fairlie had wanted to come up here, by himself. He wanted to visualize that, as it would have been.

He couldn't. It wouldn't work, he was too cold, too tired. There was nothing here but a vast ruined hall, and shattered imitation-stars below and real stars overhead, and the chill wind.

"Too long ago," he thought heavily. "Nobody can recapture a thing so long ago."

He felt a disappointment. He had thought that somehow this would bring him close to the woman whose song had lived forever. That he might almost be able to see her, up there on the balcony, singing.

And how would it have been when she sang to the stars then, and down there below amid their shining trophies the great lords and star-captains of the Vanryn listened? Surely every heart in the vast hall would have throbbed with pride as that surpassing anthem called to the stars until they seemed to lean down toward the woman to listen? Surely, surely, watching her up there with her head flung back and her silver voice wild and beautiful, you would see the shining ships going forth on the greatest adventure, the strong men who laid hold on suns, the valiant voices that mocked at space and death, the glory of a race who had desired all the universe? Surely your eyes would be wet with tears when you heard her singing?

175

And Fairlie heard that singing, as he had heard it so many times. And his eyes were wet, his heart too throbbed hard with painful pride—

A jarring sound shattered the illusion. A rude unmusical voice in a distant cry.

Fairlie opened his eyes. He was high on the stair in the great Hall, and the wind blew cold, and there was no singing, no illusion at all any longer, and then he heard the cry again.

Hagulian, shouting in a high, raw voice from outside the Hall.

Fairlie jumped to his feet, and started down the stair. He heard the others pounding across the Hall toward the doorway. When he reached the floor he ran himself, between the glowing mock-suns, after them. He ran out through the shattered doorway onto the vast terrace around the building.

DeWitt and the others were there, and Hagulian was pointing, and they were all staring.

"I knew they would follow," said Thrayn tragically to Fairlie when he saw him.

Fairlie stared. Far down there at the base of the mountain, out from it a certain distance, scattered fires had come into being. They were mere pinpoints of leaping ruddy light from up here, but they formed a circle all around the mountain, down among the scattered trees.

"All right," DeWitt said roughly, loudly. "So Thrayn's people have come after us. If they try to come up here we'll slap them back damn fast."

"They will not come up here," said Thrayn, as though he divined what DeWitt was saying. "They would not set foot here. But they will wait for us down there."

Aral whimpered and clung to Thrayn, peering down at the fires with wide, scared eyes.

"Wait, is it?" said DeWitt when Fairlie translated. "Let them wait. We'll rout them out of there when daylight comes."

He gave orders, loud and confident ones. The watch was to be doubled. The rest of them could go in and get their sleep. In the morning, they would deal with this.

176

Fairlie asked Thrayn, "Would it help any if I went down and talked to your people, explained why we're here?"

He hoped fervently that Thrayn would say, No, it wouldn't. He didn't want to go down there. But as the only one of them who could speak the language, he felt he had to make the offer. He was relieved when Thrayn shook his head.

"No—they don't care why you're here," Thrayn said. "They just want you to go, to leave Ryn, to take your ship away before you bring the Llorn here."

Fairlie could not sleep. He was cold, and he was scared. The ring of fires down there had an ominous look. He hoped DeWitt was right about routing them out of there. He hoped it very much.

At daybreak, DeWitt was on the radio to Thomason, explaining the situation. "I want the 'copters to come and flush them out of here. Buzz them, fire a few shots. They'll run."

Thomason's voice sounded worried. "And if they don't?"

"They will."

But they did not. The 'copters came droning through the yellow glare of rising Altair, and roared low down over the little knots of men around the smoking fires, and the flat crack of shots came through the roar. Back and forth went the ungainly skitter-planes, making one pass after another.

The men down there left their campfires. They ran into the scattered clumps of trees, and stayed there until the 'copters had gone. Then they came out again, and sat down again around their fires, their faces turned toward the top of the mountain.

There was a silence. They all looked at DeWitt. His face was hard and angry, but when he turned and met their gaze, he smiled.

"So they didn't scare," DeWitt said. "All right, the devil with them. We'll just let 'em wait down there and freeze their feet. They won't come up here, they're too superstitious about the Llorn. We've got a job to do and we'll do it, and let 'em wait."

Nobody answered that for a moment. The men looked at each other unhappily, and then, as though by a common impulse, they looked toward Raab and Fairlie. They had heard enough of the arguments between those two and DeWitt to know where the real opposition to DeWitt lay.

Fairlie thought, Oh, Lord, I suppose I've got to step out now and say what they expect me to, what Christensen told me to when he was dying. I knew this time would come and a lot of luck I'll have bucking against DeWitt, but I've got to.

He took the step toward DeWitt but before he could speak, Raab's incisive voice anticipated him.

"Let us be clear about this, DeWitt," said Raab, using one of his favorite phrases. Behind his eyeglasses his eyes were cool and impersonal. "Are we to stay here, in increasing danger, to continue this futile search?"

"Why, yes, we are," said DeWitt heartily. "We certainly are." And of a sudden his pretended good-humor dropped away and he said savagely, "And the hell of a scientist you are after all, Raab. You say the search will be futile. What kind of a large unscientific assumption is that? How do you *know* it will be futile?"

Raab said calmly, "I say that that is a logical estimate of the probabilities. This Hall of Suns is a monument. Nothing else. The weapons and machines and secrets that have obsessed you wouldn't ever have been here. As I've said before, they would have been down in the starports and arsenals of that city, where the Llorn destroyed them long ago."

"I agree," said Fairlie. "I think that we ought to break out of here and return to the ship."

"And *I* certainly agree," squeaked Winstedt hastily. "For God's sake, DeWitt, use your common sense. We haven't found anything, and there's no need to throw away our lives."

DeWitt looked around at their faces, and then at the other men. "You're all of the same mind?" There was a silence. "I see you are." His face was calm now, almost triumphant.

And in a sudden flash of intuition, Fairlie thought he could see into DeWitt's thinking. He was the leader. He had brought them here, to this far world, by forcing the issue. They would not have come without him and now they were scared, they wanted to quit. But *he* would never quit that easily. He would hold them to it, until success rewarded their search in spite of everything, because he was the leader.

"We stay right here," said DeWitt, deliberately. "And I want to remind you that I have a gun and you don't and that as commanding authority on this expedition I can punish mutiny." He folded his arms, and smiled at them.

Yes, thought Fairlie, I was right. He's savoring this, the strong man against the weak ones.

"How about food and water?" demanded Raab.

"We've enough for a day or so."

"And then——?"

"Then," said DeWitt, "we'll worry about it. Right now we've other things to worry about. Smith, you and Muirhead keep watch, and watch them too." His thumb jerked toward Thrayn and Aral. "The rest of you will resume the search-programs I've already outlined."

There was another silence, and the cold yellow sunlight fell upon their faces and the cold wind whispered.

Raab said slowly, "Christensen was wiser than we knew. He said that you were unbalanced, dangerous, obsessed. And you are."

"Oh, bosh," said DeWitt contemptuously. "Chris was a humanitarian in a world that can't afford humanitarians any more. And I'm no more obsessed than you are. I've just got more guts, that's all. Now get to work." And he turned his back on them and went back through the broken golden doors into the Hall.

They looked at each other, and they could find nothing to say. It was the old situation, thought Fairlie, the reasonable men who could perceive realities against the one man who refused to admit realities, but the one man would fight to the death for his obsession, and that was what gave them pause.

"He'll come to his senses before long," said Raab. "He'll have to, when the water gives out."

All that day they went on with the search-programs that not a

179

one of them now believed in. Fairlie went on with his translations, and they were ringing and splendid tributes to the Vanryn star-captains, but there was nothing in them that would satisfy DeWitt.

Thrayn and Aral sat in a shadowy corner and did nothing, and talked little. They looked crushed. They evinced no desire at all to escape, and Fairlie could guess that escape to their people down on the plain would be no escape at all.

Night came and the watchfires of the Vanryn down there blazed out in their scattered ring. The wind blew moaning through the Hall of Suns and the little mock-suns of the shattered universe lit the dark and sullen faces of the men as they ate their reduced ration and drank their bit of water and crawled into the sleeping-bags. Fairlie did not think that they would take this much longer.

Yet, incredibly, DeWitt's voice roused them in the morning and drove them back to the senseless program. Search for vaults and hidden chambers that are not there, translate secrets that are not there, rip it out, make it go.

There was a shadow of strain in DeWitt's hard face this day. Fairlie almost felt sorry for him. DeWitt must know that time was running out on him and yet he would not give up, he must keep at it or admit defeat and that he could not do.

The crisis came in mid-afternoon when the last bit of water was doled out. They drank it, and then they looked at DeWitt.

"I'd say that that does it," said Winstedt anxiously. "You see that we can't stay here any longer now, DeWitt? Surely you see that we have to break out of here now?"

"We stay," said DeWitt.

Muirhead, ordinarily the mildest and most placid of the men, spoke rapidly. "Oh, no. If you think we're going to die of thirst here just because you've gone nuts, why——"

"Nobody's going to die of thirst," DeWitt said contemptuously. "I'm going to call Thomason. I'll have the 'copters drop us food and water as long as we're here."

"And how long is that going to be—forever?" demanded

180

Fairlie. "Can the 'copters keep supplying us for a lifetime, just because you can't admit you're wrong?"

"We can get the tracs going tonight and break right out through that circle," Muirhead added. "We've got to do it."

"Anybody tries it, I'll kill him," DeWitt said quietly. "You know I mean that."

He stood there inside the broken golden doors, with the yellow shaft of light from outside outlining his stocky figure, and Fairlie knew that he gloried in this moment. He was the leader, the unyielding one, the undefeated.

DeWitt walked to the radio, and they looked after him undecidedly, all of them furious except Thrayn and Aral who huddled in their own private misery by the wall. He worked the switches and his back was to them as though he was scornful of anything they might do.

"Thomason?" he said. "Listen, I've got orders for you. What's that? Tell me later— What's that?"

Thomason's voice was squarking out of the radio. "—what I told you, a blip on the radar just now. It could be another ship coming, DeWitt—it could be another ship from Earth, only from the other side of the Curtain."

"Oh, hell, there's no ship coming, you just saw a bogey," said DeWitt impatiently.

"But—"

"I tell you, there's no ship coming. What you heard Christensen say was true enough, *I* took Fairlie's tapes to prod the project along, there wasn't any spy. There isn't any ship, either. Now listen. We've got a problem here."

Fairlie listened and he felt the defiance and the anger drain out of him. He had a dull feeling that it wasn't any use. His premonition had been right. One way or another, DeWitt would keep them here until it was too late to go.

He felt cold and beaten. The sunlight from the doorway had darkened, as though it was clouding heavily outside, and he looked up through the high opening in the loftiest dome and saw dark shadow across the heavens, shadow that seemed to pour

181

down through the opening and deepen and darken in the great Hall and dim the shining little suns. And still the shadows darkened, and DeWitt kept talking crisply, and it was icy cold . . .

Aral screamed suddenly, in a voice that was hardly human.

She had leaped to her feet and her face was white and distorted by a terror that made it almost animal-like. She pointed to the dome, to the deepening shadows, and she cried out indistinguishably.

Thrayn cried out too. Then the two of them, scrambling, slipping wildly in their terror, bolted out through the golden doors.

"Catch them, they're trying to get away!" cried DeWitt furiously. "Oh, damn it!"

He dropped the mike of the radio and plunged through the doors. Shocked, not comprehending the sudden outburst, Fairlie ran out after him, with the others following.

On the great stone terrace, Aral had slipped and DeWitt had grabbed her arm. Thrayn was trying to tear away his grip but DeWitt held onto Aral with his left hand around her wrist, and grappled Thrayn with his free arm.

"Help me!" DeWitt yelled angrily. "They've gone crazy."

Fairlie could not move to help anyone. He was too stunned by the sudden and inexplicable change that seemed to have come over everything.

The air had darkened as though in an eclipse. But it was nothing high in the sky that brought this darkness. It was a weird deepening of shadow in the air all about them, cutting off the light, cutting off all the heat of the sun, seeming to swirl and flow about them slowly, ever deeper, ever darker.

He could barely see the plain below, but he could make out the figures of those men of Thrayn's people who had besieged them. They were fleeing now, running away from the mountain and the Hall of Suns, ludicrous little moving puppets. From down there among them came a thin, far cry, a word, and Aral was screeching that word over and over again.

"The Llorn!"

And Thrayn, his voice choked with rage and terror, cried, "Let her go—the Llorn are coming! The shadowed ones!"

Fairlie felt a great throb of painful doubt, of surprise, and he saw DeWitt and the struggling Thrayn and Aral as though through darkening waters, and he did not know quite what was happening. It couldn't be what they said.

Thrayn tore loose, and Fairlie started forward again. DeWitt released Aral and grabbed for Thrayn with both hands. Aral's hand dipped into her garment and came out again with something, and then the knife that Muirhead had lost dug deep into DeWitt's back.

Fairlie yelled and ran through the icy shadows. Thrayn and Aral had leaped away and were gone down the roadway to the plain, running like rabbits.

DeWitt stood there and looked puzzledly at Fairlie when Fairlie reached him. "She hit me," he said thickly. "She hit me in the back with something."

He did not fall but he crumpled a little at the knees and Fairlie tried to catch him but all he could do was to ease him down clumsily onto the stone, on his side.

DeWitt looked into the darkening shadows with no interest in anything at all any more. "She hit me," he said and died.

The shadows darkened and darkened and it was cold now as though the breath of outer space was upon them. They could not even see clearly each other's faces as they looked at each other from where they had bent over DeWitt. And still the strange haze chilled and deepened.

It was then that a voice, a whispering, carrying voice, came to them through the dark obscurity. It spoke in the old Vanryn and it said, "Let those of authority and knowledge among you come to us."

They looked at the blurs of each other's faces and then Winstedt giggled and said in a high, hysterical voice, "You know, I think they were right. I think the Llorn have come."

25

FAIRLIE STOOD in the cold semi-darkness, with Raab beside him and Winstedt trembling and gasping somewhere behind them, and looked at the three dark shadowed shapes in front of them and heard the husky, whispering voice, and he thought, Isn't it wonderful how adaptable humans are, they can stand anything.

Well, almost anything . . .

If they try to go into my mind I can't stand that.

Don't think about that. This isn't a nightmare like those in the ship. You are Doctor Robert Fairlie of Boston in Massachusetts and you are a respected young scholar and you are talking to the Llorn.

To three of them, anyway. Three dark shapes who somehow shroud themselves in shadows. They are thick, they are upright, they are somehow manlike, they are not men. All right, so they're not, this can still be a straight man-to-not-man talk.

That isn't funny, that's the edge of hysteria. For God's sake keep hold of yourself.

He kept hold. He stood and looked at the three dark shadowy figures, and it seemed to him that he had stood like this for hours. And yet it had been only minutes, really, since he and Raab and Winstedt had scaredly, hesitantly, answered that summoning whispering and had gone into the darkened Hall and through the dimmed mock-suns to the shadows in the far side where the summoners waited.

184

He was cold, he was shivering. Not with fear but with just plain icy cold. The warmth of the sun had gone with its light. Chill shadow wrapped all the Hall. Somewhere in that shadow, whatever craft the Llorn had come in must be waiting. Somewhere, there might be other Llorn. You couldn't see, the protective darkness the Llorn carried with them was too effective a shield. No wonder Thrayn and Aral called them "the shadowed ones." Thrayn and Aral—did they get clear? Probably. What difference does it make now? But what a hell of a way for DeWitt to die.

"You are not listening," said the husky whisper, speaking the old Vanryn language slowly and tonelessly. "The others cannot understand, and you do not listen."

Fairlie tried to get the stiffness out of his throat and tongue, and answer. He needed to talk, for all he was worth. These were the Llorn, who had destroyed a city and broken a great race, and he thought it quite likely that they would destroy him too, but he had to talk against it while he could.

"I am listening now," he said in the old Vanryn language. "I hear you."

"It has always been true of the Vanryn," said the Llorn. "They *would* not listen."

There was an impatience in that slight emphasis that somehow humanized the shadowy figures, and gave Fairlie more courage to speak. "We are not of the Vanryn," he said. "We come from Earth, a distant world, a distant star."

"We know. You are the far children of the Vanryn, grown now to lust for stars. Surely you are worthy of your parents!"

From behind Fairlie, Winstedt plucked at him with a trembling hand and whispered, "Ask them if they'll show themselves, Fairlie. We ought to see what they're like. Biologically, I mean."

Fairlie felt a fleeting admiration for Winstedt. The man was a soft self-seeker. But he was also a scientist.

Fairlie said in English, "For God's sake be quiet."

The quiet whisper of the Llorn who spoke—Fairlie thought it

was the middle one of the three, but how could you tell when you couldn't see them through the shadows?—reached him.

"We have watched and warded space for a long time, lest the Vanryn go forth in it again. We saw when you did so, we looked into your ship—yes, into your minds. We saw that you knew we had forbidden the Vanryn to go to space, yet you scoffed at and ignored our edict."

Now, Fairlie thought desperately, was the time to explain, to make excuses. To tell how they had discovered the old knowledge by chance, how they had been unable to believe that the Llorn edict was other than legend, how it was not their fault.

That was the thing to say but he could not say it. There had risen in him a completely irrational resentment and anger that he could not for the life of him control. He did not know whether it was because hysteria was conquering his common sense, but he had to voice that resentment.

"Then no one must ever go to the stars because the Llorn have claimed them all?" he said.

From one of the Llorn came a sound that was almost a sigh. "The Vanryn strain has not changed," said the whispering voice. "Always, you impute to others the motives that you have yourselves." And the whisper came louder. "You say that the Llorn claim all the stars. Are there Llorn upon your world?"

"No," said Fairlie.

"Were there Llorn here on Ryn?"

"No."

"Is there a great Llorn empire encompassing the galaxy? The answer is No, again. We Llorn desire no conquests. We have our own far world and we want no other."

Fairlie said skeptically, with anger still supporting him, "Then why did you war against the Vanryn and break them, long ago?"

"Because," came the answer, "the Vanryn *did* desire to conquer all the universe. Their hands could never have been filled enough. They would have seeded all the stars with their own stock and no other race would have been allowed to arise. We did not fear them—we are too old and powerful a people to have

186

such fear. But we could not allow Vanryn conquest to frustrate the natural evolution of countless worlds."

"You fought the Vanryn, just for that?" Fairlie said incredulously. "Just for a philosophical ideal?"

"You do not believe. The Vanryn of old could not believe, either, or understand. We had not impeded their evolution, their rise upon this world. And in turn we would not allow them to impede the development of other peoples whose various qualities of mind could enrich the universe."

And as Fairlie still stood silent and incredulous, the quiet whisper said, "We shall make you understand. Look upon us."

A painful constriction seized Fairlie's heart. The shadows that wrapped the three Llorn were lifting.

He saw the Llorn.

Raab sucked in his breath and said nothing.

Winstedt, behind him, whispered raptly, "Look at that. Mammalian possibly, or perhaps marsupial or even oviparous. Humanoid superficially, but of a different stock completely."

Fairlie only mechanically heard the enrapt biologist's speculation. Humanoid, superficially. Manlike. Not men, but manlike.

Bipeds, not with long thin legs but with short thick ones, and short thick arms, and short thick bodies. Their skin dark and hairless, their bodies quite unclothed and without perceptible sexual organs. Their heads and faces are heads and faces, broad, neckless, wide mouths, wide nostril-openings, quiet eyes that have no pupils, and that have the wisdom of ages in them and— oh God—the things those eyes must have looked upon that I will never know, and I am afraid, afraid, afraid . . .

The whispering voice came from the wide mouth of the center one of the Llorn.

"You see that we came from far different stock than the Vanryn, than your ancestors. Yet everywhere, on every world that has life, if not impeded intelligent life will develop toward the humanoid form that is most versatile and adaptable. In the universe, there are many kinds of men. Yet had the Vanryn had their way there would only have been one kind, dominating all others.

187

"We would not allow that. On each world, we told them, life must be allowed to develop in its own way. They must not carry conquest across the stars. Here, in this very Hall long ago, our envoys warned them that if they did not withdraw from their course of conquest, we would force them back."

And again, Fairlie heard the sound that was almost a sigh, a whisper of infinite regret.

"They would not withdraw. They laughed at our warning. And so we Llorn had to use the thing we hate most. Force. Warfare, carried across the galaxy to force the Vanryn back to their own world. And once they were here, to destroy their ships and forbid them to fly the stars again. We did the thing, and the galaxy has developed in peace since then."

There was a pregnant pause, and the next words struck Fairlie's ear like slow notes of doom.

"But now, after all this time, the seed of the Vanryn has come forth again to space. We have been aware of it. And we have debated our course. Should we strike again, to keep the sons of the Vanryn out of space?"

Again the little pause, and life or death hung upon it and Fairlie waited, the palms of his hands slippery with sweat despite the cold. The broad, calm faces, the deep, strange eyes, looked at him.

"We have made our decision," whispered the Llorn. "We hate force and war. We cannot bring ourselves again to use them. So we will not interfere if you surge again across the stars. But before you do, sons of the Vanryn, we bring you a warning! We warn you that if you go to space as conquerors, you will destroy yourselves, for always force breeds force and conquest breeds rebellion."

And of a sudden the eyes that looked into Fairlie's seemed to grow enormous, to become vast blacknesses into which he was falling, and the whisper sounded like thunder in his mind.

In his mind! He knew that they had invaded his mind, that they were taking control, he fought against it, he heard Raab and Winstedt cry out and knew that they too were fighting against that

188

invasion. But it was in vain, he couldn't resist that mental assault, he was in darkness, in the cosmic abyss, and the voice of the Llorn rang across it.

"Look well before you make your choice, oh sons of the Vanryn! See what you choose if you go to the stars as conquerors —that which happened long ago and has haunted all the stars, that which will happen again. Look!"

Fairlie looked. He was above the whole vast panorama and glitter of the galaxy, he was like a god looking down on it, he could see it all at once and in detail, and yet all the time he knew that his godlike vision was only put into his mind from outside.

He saw the proud, shining fleets of the Vanryn put out from Ryn, great argosies of conquest outbound for distant suns. They swept grandly through the starways, they hardily plumbed the ultra-dimensional depths of nothingness and made worldfall on strange and beautiful planets under vari-colored suns. They planted their people on world after world, and ever on they went, these men who desired all a universe. And when their fleets came homing from the stars, the pride and the glory of the Vanryn were like a flame upon this world.

Time went by, centuries, thousands of years, in the tick of a second. And now far out amid the stars there was a crackling of light, a stabbing and slashing of beams or forces only half visible. It seemed to Fairlie that he looked closer without effort, and he saw now that it was an unthinkable battle-line that flashed and crackled out there in the darkness, the shining ships of the Vanryn grappling with shadow-wrapped craft that struck them, and struck them again. In the Vanryn ships men died like heroes, and it was in vain, they were driven back, ever back, by the shadowed ships.

On world after alien world the bases of the Vanryn fought fierce defensive actions, but shadowed fleets came down upon them and smote them and they were silent and still. In perilous passes between gigantic blazing suns, in the tangling, glowing depths of tenuous nebulae, in the tenebrous reaches of dark cosmic clouds that flamed to sudden glory with the glare of the battle, the Vanryn fought, but the shadow-sheathed ships hounded them, driving them back toward Altair and the little gleaming globe of Ryn. And then there was a nightmare glimpse of a vast starport, the last citadel of the Vanryn power, leaping to light in the flame of its own destruction. And then there was darkness.

"Look well!" rang the voice in Fairlie's mind. "Look upon Ryn and the people of Ryn as they are today, and be sure that if you go forth to space in conquest, the long road will have the self-same end."

Darkness, and silence now. And cold. Fairlie felt very cold, and the stone floor was like ice against his face.

His face. He had fallen, then? He raised his head. There were no Llorn. There was no more shadow. He was in the corner of the dusky Hall of Suns, and the little mock-suns of the shattered miniature universe shone brightly, and there was nothing else here except Raab and Winstedt, wild-eyed, staring, scrambling shakily to their feet, helping him up.

"They're gone?" whispered Winstedt.

"I think so," said Raab. "Yes." He looked at them. "You heard it, you saw? A warning and a vision. My God, what a vision." After a moment he asked, "What did they say, before?"

Fairlie told them.

After a moment, Raab said, "So that is the side of the story that we never knew, the side the Vanryn did not tell."

"Was it true?"

"God knows. Would they come so far to tell a lie? I think it was true. And I think their warning was a true one."

There was the sound of voices, scared, high-pitched, doubtful, as Hagulian and Smith and Muirhead came through the little shining suns.

"Doctor Raab? Doctor Fairlie?" they called, fearfully. Then they saw them, and came running with clumsy haste. "For Christ's sake, what happened? There was the shadow, colder and colder, and then the shadow lifted, and there was nothing, and—"

Raab interrupted. He had found his eyeglasses and put them

on and he was making an attempt to be matter-of-fact. "Christensen's dead, and now DeWitt's dead," he said. "As senior scientist of this expedition, I'm taking command."

Nobody objected to that.

"We're getting out of here," Raab said. "We're going back to the ship, and we're leaving Ryn. If we're lucky we'll get back to Earth."

"We'll make it, sure we will," said Hagulian eagerly. "But what I want to know is about the Llorn, if it *was* them."

Raab said, "We'll tell the whole world that, when the time comes. I don't think it will be for a while. I think they'll find it wiser at home to keep this whole voyage quiet as long as they can. But when the time comes, when it's necessary, we have a warning to convey."

They went outside where the others waited. Raab gave orders. The men began hastily gathering the packs together, needing no urging at all.

They went out into the cold sunshine, and the body of DeWitt still lay there. It seemed to Fairlie that there was a frown of puzzlement upon the hard brown face.

"What about him?" Hagulian asked Raab.

Fairlie answered that. "There's plenty of fallen rock inside. We can build a cairn over him."

"That'll take time," said Hagulian doubtfully.

Raab looked at Fairlie and then he said, "We'll take the time."

The cairn grew, and the puzzled brown face was covered from their sight. And Fairlie thought, You were a bastard, DeWitt, but you deserve a decent resting-place here, you labored hard enough to get here.

He had learned something, Fairlie thought. A man could be a bastard and still be great. DeWitt had been limited, single-minded, a blind fanatic, not half the man that Christensen had been, in most ways. And yet it was DeWitt who had lied and schemed and argued and dragged them to the stars. Whether for good or ill, it was DeWitt who had done it.

For good or ill—who knew? He would take the warning of

191

the Llorn back to Earth but would it be heeded? He didn't know. He didn't know at all.

Fairlie turned his back upon the cairn and followed Raab and the others down the side of the mountain.